A Veil of Execration

Maelana Nightingale

CONTENTS

Dear Not-So-Gentle Reader,

First, let me thank you for picking up A *Veil of Execration*. I hope you brought a stiff drink, a rosary, and maybe a therapist on retainer. Because this isn't a sweet love story with hand-holding and picnics. This is the kind of book where the picnic basket contains zip ties, the wine is laced with menace, and the blanket is already stained with blood.

Leon is not a cinnamon roll. He's not even a burnt croissant. He's arsenic wrapped in French leather with a gun tucked into his belt and a knife under your pillow. And Savannah? She probably *should* run, but instead she trips, moans, and thanks him for chaining her to the altar.

So, before you wander in unsuspecting, here's your **menu of depravity** (also known as content warnings):

- Graphic death, murder, and violence (artistic blood-splatter included)

- Unnegotiated Dominant/submissive dynamic (no contracts, no safewords, just Leon being Leon)

- A sizeable age gap (38/22, or as Leon would say: *"old enough to be man enough for her"*)

- Edge play & primal play (if you don't know, you'll learn)

- Blood play, knife play, gun play (basically if it cuts, bleeds, or goes *bang*, Leon thinks it's a sex toy)

- Orgasm control (she begs, he denies, everyone suffers beautifully)

- Breeding kink (with a side of birth control tampering)

- Stalking (the obsessive, obsessive kind—he's basically her personal shadow with a murder habit)

- And probably a few other sins I forgot to confess

If any of the above makes you clutch your pearls, consider this your polite exit.

If instead you need to make sure your battery-operated boyfriend is charged before turning the next page—welcome home.

With blood, wine, and at least a little French profanity,
Maelana ~ Stay Naughty

You can listen along to the playlist I've curated for this book on either my YouTube or Spotify

For the good girls who want to be stolen.
For the bad girls who want to be kept.
This book is for every sinner who ever whispered *take me* instead of *save me*.
For every heart that beats faster in danger, and every soul that knows ruin can feel like home.

I
FIRST LOOK

LEON

MONEY SMELLS THE SAME, no matter who it comes from. But the men who hand it over always reek of something else—sweat, desperation, sin. Hale stinks of all three.

He leans forward across the mahogany desk like we're equals. Like I won't slit his throat if the mood shifts. I let him believe it. Although, sometimes fear sweetens the contract.

"My daughter is getting married," he says, like it's supposed to mean something to me. I don't blink. Just light another cigarette and wait.

"She doesn't get to choose who she's marrying," Hale mutters, almost like it's a point of pride. Then he clears his throat. "But I do need to make sure the bastard doesn't embarrass the bloodline before he's buried in it."

He drums thick, liver-spotted fingers against the glass. "Her fiancé—Carson Gardner—comes from good money, decent stock. But... I need assurance."

There it is.

I exhale smoke into the quiet and let it coil around the word. "Assurance?"

"Beyond the normal background check—things the normal investigators didn't find. Discreet." He swallows. "If there's anything off about him, I want to know. I won't let her marry trash."

That's rich coming from a man who made his fortune laundering blood. I've cleaned up after men like him for years—southern tycoons with more secrets than soul, smiling through their teeth while their daughters rot behind estate gates. Hale is no different. He wears wealth like a shield and pretends it's virtue.

But I've seen his kind weep when their bodies start to fail—when the devil they paid off stops answering the phone.

There was one, years ago, just like this. Pretty little heiress promised off to a man twice her age—abusive, rich, and politically useful. Her father hired me to 'correct the situation.'

I did. But I sent the daughter into hiding first.

She didn't thank me. Didn't need to. I didn't do it for her.

I did it because I don't like men who break the things they claim to protect.

Still, I nod once. Cold. Calculated.

"How discreet?" I ask.

His lips twitch. "I don't want her involved. She can't know. She's... fragile."

I don't give a fuck about fragile. But I file that word away.

"Timeline?"

"Three weeks until the wedding." His eyes flicker. "He's staying in one of our penthouse suites. You'll have full access."

Of course I will. I always do.

He pushes a folder across the desk. "You'll find his itinerary, known associates, security patterns. Do what you do, Mr. Mercier."

I stand, button my coat, and slide the folder under one arm. Hale holds out a hand like we're closing a business deal. I stare at it until he lets it drop.

"Mr. Mercier," he calls after me as I reach the door. "Be thorough."

I look back, just once. "Always am."

***

I READ THE FOLDER in the back seat of the limo on the drive back to the suite Hale booked for me. Neatly labeled tabs. Chronological dossiers. Paper-clipped surveillance reports. All curated to look clean. It takes me six hours to burn through the lies.

Not because it's not hidden well—because it's hidden with money. That's the thing with men like Carson. They don't bother to bury the bones. They just pay someone else to step over them.

First, I pull hotel surveillance from the week before. Takes a burner call and a cash drop to the night manager, but I get what I need. Footage of Carson dragging a girl by the arm into an elevator. She stumbles. He yanks her harder. Her wrist bends in a way that tells me it would have stayed purple for weeks.

She never left—not on camera.

Then I call in a favor—Rex, a hacker I use when I want more to burn someone with than I can get myself. He scrapes Carson's cloud backups and finds voice memos—muffled screams, panicked whispers. One file is nothing but the sound of crying. No talking. No music. Just crying... for seven minutes.

Mixed into the cloud cache is a compressed folder of images labeled "*Fundraiser_Archive*." Inside, tucked between event shots and boring publicity stills, is a photo that doesn't belong with the others.

Savannah Hale.

It's from a formal gala a few months ago—her father's charity event in New Orleans. She's mid-step, holding a champagne flute, flanked by two society matrons I barely register.

Because I only see her.

Her face is turned just slightly toward the camera. Eyes wide, mouth caught between a practiced smile and a visible flinch. You have to look closely to see it—but it's there. The way she's holding her body, like every part of her has been taught to yield without breaking. Like someone who has never learned to scream. I wonder if she even knows she wants to.

It's just a photo. Frozen. Staged.

I stare at it longer than anything else in the file.

But then I move on—Carson Gardner has a type. And a pattern.

And now he has a problem.

Carson Gardner isn't just trash. He's fucking rot.

His finances are shaky at best. Hale thinks he's marrying his daughter into old money, but Carson is bleeding debt from gambling markers, real estate scams, and offshore shell companies propped up by men who don't forget unpaid favors.

One of them is a known associate of the DiLuca syndicate.

That's problem number one.

Problem number two stinks worse. Hidden under charity invoices and offshore "consulting" fees is a string of wire transfers that trace back to a shuttered nightclub in Macau. The kind that didn't close because of bankruptcy—but because someone found a thirteen-year-old girl dead in a locked VIP room. And I'm not surprised when I learn who was last seen with her.

Carson wasn't arrested.

He was "unreachable."

Putain de merde.

I reach for my second cigarette. Light it off the end of the first. The deeper I dig, the filthier it gets. Sex tourism. Stimulant trafficking. Fake rehab clinics used to cycle victims. Photos tagged and deleted from burner socials—girls that look like Savannah, but younger. Bent over penthouse furniture or gagged and glassy-eyed.

He's not just scum. He's fucking dangerous. And reckless. And worst of all? He's stupid enough to think no one's watching.

I close the laptop. Stretch my neck until it pops. Then pull out my knife, just to feel the weight of it in my hand.

Men like him don't deserve trials—they deserve men like me.

***

I CATCH MY FIRST live glimpse of Savannah Hale through a zoom lens from the thirty-sixth floor. The ballroom is draped in crystal and gold, all fake smiles and Southern grandeur. But she doesn't belong to it. Not really.

She's seated next to Carson—flanked, more like. Her spine straight. Her shoulders held in quiet tension that most men would miss. Not me.

She's twenty-two, the file said. But she carries herself older, heavier. Like she's been holding her breath for years.

Blonde. Not the bright, perky kind. No—hers is ash gold, pulled into a loose chignon, a few soft tendrils trailing against her collarbone. She's wearing ivory silk that hugs her waist, the neckline daring but demure. Every inch of her screams polish. Except her eyes.

Through the lens, I watch her laugh at something Carson says. The sound doesn't reach me, but I can read the truth in her face. It's a lie. Her lips part. Teeth flash. But her eyes stay hollow. Fixed on some far-off place. That's not joy. That's performance. Habit. Survival.

She tilts her head when she laughs, but it's mechanical—more of a twitch than a reaction. Her fingers twist around the stem of her champagne flute, knuckles whitening every time Carson leans closer. There's a tremor in her pinky. Controlled. Masked. But it's there. She's barely breathing, like inhaling too deeply might draw attention.

I shift in my chair. Clench the zoom lens tighter until my knuckles creak.

She's not beautiful in the way society likes to photograph. She's beautiful in the way wolves dream of moonlight. Pale. Untouchable. On the edge of vanishing.

I wonder how she'd look on her knees. Not broken. Not begging. Just bare—undone in that silk, eyes wide and waiting, mouth parted like she doesn't know if she's meant to moan or pray.

I wonder if she's ever been kissed without flinching. If she's ever been touched like she matters. If anyone has ever made her feel anything other than used or owned or promised off like a fucking property deal.

I bet not. I bet every man in her life—starting with her father—has taken and twisted and justified it.

But I wouldn't just take. I'd unmake her—slowly, exquisitely, until the only thing left inside her is the shape of me. I'd dismantle every lie she's been taught about love and safety, then rebuild her with my hands, my mouth, my violence. I'd burn her clean and make her holy in the ruin.

I'd make her forget her own name before I let her forget mine. Because when I'm finished, there won't be a single inch of her untouched by my devotion. She'll beg—not for release, but for permanence.

And I'll give it to her. In scars. In bruises. In vows.

Carson puts a possessive hand on her thigh under the table. She doesn't recoil. Doesn't flinch. But her shoulders tense half a degree. Her gaze fixes on the chandelier above them. Like she's trying to float away.

My jaw ticks. I picture slicing the fucker's hand off at the wrist. Letting him bleed out over the dessert course.

I bet she wouldn't even blink.

Because she's already gone. And no one at that table has noticed.

But I have.

Ma poupée. All painted up, all mine.

Carson's hand on her thigh grazes higher under the table. She doesn't move. But she blinks—slow, mechanical. Like she's disassociating just to get through dinner.

And that's the moment it happens.

That's the final fucking trigger.

Something about her has been calling to me. And now—now it's a siren-song, a string pulling taut that I can't ignore. I've never felt this way about any woman.

Is this that love at first sight shit people talk about?

I've seen enough women like her in the files of the men I've buried. I've watched too many go numb before they die.

Not this one. Not her.

She doesn't know it yet, but I've already chosen.

I've fucked more women than I can count—one night, no names, no attachments. Wet heat and forgotten faces. I *don't* feel things.

Not like this. Not ever.

But watching her? Through glass and distance and silence? It's like a blade under my skin. Slow. Precise.

She isn't just another mark. She isn't disposable. She's *mine*.

This job just changed.

Je vais peindre les murs avec son sang.

I close the camera case, tuck the lens into its padded slot, and light another cigarette on the walk back to the suite. Every step buzzes with new purpose.

She's in this hotel. Just floors below. Caged in pearls and protocol and expectation. I wonder how soon I can get closer.

Days? Hours?

Can I get her alone?

Will I have to take her?

Or will she come willingly, confused and trembling, because something in her already recognizes what I am?

I've already planned the next move before I reach the elevator. I'll watch her again—up close this time. Maybe I'll whisper her name, just once, see if she shivers.

She'll never say "I do" to him.

Because I want her.

And what I want?

I fucking take.

2

SOMETHING BORROWED

SAVANNAH

Twenty-two days until I become Mrs. Carson Gardner.

Twenty-two days until the cage slams shut.

I wake to birdsong and the cloying scent of gardenia. The windows are cracked just enough to let in the manicured breeze. Everything in this room is soft, floral, and calculated—cream drapes, blush silk pillows, a vanity too delicate to hold anything heavier than lip gloss and expectation.

This isn't a bedroom. It's a showroom. A southern fairytale frozen in time. My mother's idea of perfection. A place where girls grow into wives, not women.

I slip out of bed and pad barefoot across the polished floor, my nightgown whispering around my thighs. The chill of the morning air kisses my skin, and for a moment, I pretend it's real. That I'm free. That I can walk out of this room, this house, this name—and never look back.

But then I catch my reflection in the mirror—and flinch. She looks like someone I should envy—polished, poised, demure. But I don't recognize her. She's a mask sewn from obedience, stitched together by every rule I was forced to swallow. A girl designed to be possessed. Not seen. Not heard. Just displayed.

My mother says I glow with bridal grace.

I think it's just the resignation.

I remember being fourteen, locked in a dressing room for three hours because I refused to wear the debutante gown she chose. I cried until my throat cracked. She waited until the tears dried, then reapplied my lipstick and told me to be grateful for the life I was born into.

Grateful. For this.

I pick up the silk robe from the back of the chair and shrug it on, tying the sash tight enough to feel it. One small act of control. One small reminder that I still have a body beneath all this lace and legacy.

A body I don't even own. I'm borrowing it. I'm living a borrowed life.

My first kiss was scheduled during a photo op. My first orgasm came from a vibrator I stole and then smuggled into a boarding school summer program outside of London, hidden in a bottle that was supposed to be lotion. I've never had enough freedom to have sex with *anyone*, but my parents had an IUD placed when I was seventeen anyway.

My first taste of rebellion was a midnight drive to New Orleans with a tequila-high impulse to get a tattoo. I didn't make it past the courtyard of a French Quarter bar before a Hale family security officer hauled me back into the black SUV and drove me home without a word.

Then I had to face my mother.

The sunroom is where she does her best work—surrounded by lemon curd, lace gloves, and soft piano music piped through hidden speakers. The woman doesn't need to raise her voice to gut you. Not when she has shame and china teacups.

That morning, she delivered a lesson on legacy, shame, and the currency of my reputation. Optics and image are of utmost importance.

Control.

They call it tradition.

I call it a fucking prison.

My phone buzzes on the dresser—a message from Carson. *Running late. Again.* No apology. Just a photo of a watch and a stupid wink emoji. He once called me "decor," like I was part of the table setting. I think he meant it as a compliment.

I don't reply.

He'll show up eventually, flash those white teeth, kiss my cheek with bourbon breath, and call me "babe" like it's a punchline.

I used to flinch. Now I just fold.

That's what good girls do. What good wives *must* do.

Today is some sort of garden brunch. Another event on the pre-wedding circus tour. I think this one's for the investors—Carson's partners in whatever blood-soaked business he's laundering through real estate this week.

Daddy said to smile. To wear the yellow dress—the one that makes me look dainty and innocent, not sexy.

So I do.

Optics.

It's the same shade they made me wear to the summer garden gala when I was sixteen. Back when I still hoped someone might notice the panic behind my smile. Back when I still believed in escape.

The dress hangs on the back of my closet door like it's mocking me—lemon chiffon with flutter sleeves and a neckline that makes my collarbones look fragile. I put it on without thinking. Hook the tiny pearls into my ears. Sweep a neutral gloss across my mouth.

Perfect.

I leave my room with one last glance in the mirror.

The girl looking back at me is beautiful. Ethereal. Fragile.

But she's not real. She's packaging. A doll in a glass case, primped and posed.

And today, she'll be paraded like a claimed prize—no longer ripe for the highest bidder. Or the hungriest wolf.

***

THE GARDEN IS ALREADY filling with silk and secrets by the time I step outside.

A string quartet plays beneath a rented tent. Staff in pressed linen circulate with trays of pomegranate mimosas. The air smells like money and magnolias, sharp with heat and honeyed lies.

From the far edge of the property comes the sharp crack of a shotgun, the faint metallic tang of burning gunpowder drifting on the breeze. Men's voices carry—deep, jovial, competitive—someone calls pull, and another shot follows.

I've grown up with that soundtrack. Sunday skeet shooting with Daddy's friends, their tailored jackets dusted with powder, safeties clicking off like punctuation. I know the scent of cleaning solvent, the weight of a double-barrel over my arm, the thrill of hitting a clay pigeon and the pressure to pretend I enjoyed it.

I walk with my hands folded at my waist, like I was taught.

Smile just enough.

Blink slowly.

Tilt your chin when they speak.

My mother flits between guests in a pale pink sheath dress, her smile gleaming like a weapon. She nods toward me once. That means she approves.

I stand under the shade of a camellia tree, tuning out the chatter. Some finance man from Charleston is talking about hedge funds. Someone else jokes about offshore accounts like it's cocktail banter.

And then I feel it.

An unmistakable shift in air pressure. Like the moment before a storm breaks. Like lightning licking too close to skin.

I glance up—and there he is.

Not Carson. Not anyone I recognize.

He's standing near the edge of the tent, all shadow and precision. A dark suit, too sharp for the garden setting, clings to broad shoulders and a lean, hard frame that has to be at least six-foot-two. The cut is European—tailored to hint at strength and power, not flash.

His jaw is razor-sharp, mouth unsmiling, and there's a day's worth of dark stubble shadowing the edges. He has the kind of face sculpted from cruelty and control, made handsome not by softness but by symmetry and severity.

Older, definitely—mid-to-late thirties at least—but not in a way that detracts or makes me estimate less of him. If anything, it makes him more dangerous. More certain. More experienced. An earpiece coils discreetly behind his right ear. His hands are clasped behind his back like he's guarding something—or preparing to strike. Sunglasses hide his eyes, but not the weight of his stare.

He radiates danger. Discipline. Violence, barely leashed.

I know he's watching me.

I know it the same way you know when someone just flicked off a safety on a gun behind you.

My breath catches, shallow and stupid. He should scare the shit out of me. Men like him usually do. But instead, I'm curious. Drawn in like a moth too smart to burn but too tired to care.

I force myself to look away. Pick up a glass from a passing tray. Sip. Swallow. Act like my pulse isn't sprinting.

He doesn't move. He just watches.

One of Daddy's men? Maybe security?

I don't recognize him.

I try not to look again.

But I do.

And this time, he tilts his head and smirks. Like I'm a puzzle. Like he's already halfway through solving me.

The sun glints off his sunglasses. But I can feel what's behind them.

Heat.

Calculation.

Hunger.

My skin prickles.

Someone bumps into me, and I drop my gaze. The spell snaps.

I spend the rest of the brunch avoiding him without being obvious. But I feel him. And every time I turn, he's still there.

Still watching.

***

THE EVENT WINDS DOWN under a golden haze. Most of the guests have moved indoors or into smaller, more purposeful groups—carving out business deals between sips of champagne and mentions of my name.

Carson finally arrived halfway through, loud and red-faced, with apologies that didn't match his grin. He's in the parlor now, drinking with my father and pretending to care about my virtue while they auction off my future.

I slip away before anyone can corner me.

The house is blessedly quiet. Cool, dim, untouched by the sun. I take the long hallway that leads toward the rear library, hoping to hide for five minutes. Maybe ten.

My heels click against the marble. I pause to breathe. To feel something besides the tight, artificial sweetness of the past few hours.

Then I round the corner—and stop.

He's there. The man from the tent. The one in the tailored suit with the eyes I couldn't see—but now I can.

They're ice-blue. Sharp. Unforgiving. Not empty, but precise. Like scalpels. Like the crisp air in winter. Like he sees everything, and cares about none of it.

Not just watching now—waiting. Blocking the hallway like a challenge, or an invitation. I don't know who he is, but every nerve in my body recognizes him as dangerous. Important. And undeniably real.

Those eyes should make me flinch. Should send me running.

But instead, they pin me in place.

And I think—*I want to see what he does next.*

He's standing halfway down the corridor, backlit by the slanting afternoon sun, hands still behind his back. Still watching me.

And it's just us.

He doesn't move. Doesn't speak.

My heartbeat stutters. My body tenses—but not in fear. Not exactly. More like excitement.

I should turn around. Walk away.

I don't.

I take a step toward him.

He tilts his head again, slow, deliberate. Like he's memorizing me, or like he already has.

My voice comes out thinner than I want. "You're not security, are you?"

His mouth curves—barely. The ghost of a smirk.

He walks toward me with the precision of a predator who knows he doesn't need to run.

When he stops, he's close enough that I can smell him—clean and dark. Not cologne. Something colder. Metal. Leather. Gun oil, maybe.

He leans in, just enough to speak low and quiet, his voice laced with a faint French accent that grazes the words like silk over a blade.

"You deserve better than this circus, *ma colombe.*"

And then he turns, just like that, and walks away.

Gone.

Leaving me breathing too hard and trembling like I imagined it.

But I didn't.

I'll remember his voice long after tonight.

And worse—I *think I'll crave it.*

✳✳✳

I CAN'T SLEEP.

I lie in bed with the covers twisted around my thighs, skin hot and restless. The windows are shut now, the garden quiet. But my body is still humming like it remembers his presence. Like it wants more. It's still trembling under the echo of his voice.

My hand slips beneath the hem of my nightgown. I tell myself I'm not thinking about him. But I am. Not Carson. Not any of the plastic men in pressed suits.

Him.

The shadow. The voice. That faint French accent that curled around his words like smoke. The ice-blue eyes that sliced through me like glass. The scent of gun oil and sin. The ghost of his breath near my ear. And the weight of his age—experience—like he's seen things. Done things.

Things he might do to me.

I shouldn't be touching myself to the memory of a stranger. I shouldn't be aching like this at all.

But there's something in me that wants to be seen. Ruined. Broken open, exposed, and still chosen.

I arch under my own fingers, chasing something I don't really have a name for. Something that tastes like defiance and feels like a promise. My breath stutters. My hips lift. And when I come, it's quiet—but not gentle. It's raw and animalistic.

And afterward, I stare at the ceiling, hollow and full at the same time. My thighs are damp. My pulse still trips.

He didn't touch me. Didn't even say my name.

But I feel marked.

Claimed.

And for the first time in a long time... I realize it's not just that he made me feel wanted. It's that he made me feel—*anything at all.*

I don't feel numb.

I feel excited.

I feel *wanted.*

3
OBJECTIONS

LEON

She was even more intoxicating up close.

The house had been too quiet. Too staged. And when she appeared—alone, heels clicking over marble like the slow tick of a countdown—it was almost too easy. Like fate wanted her to walk straight into my hands.

She didn't recognize me. Not in the traditional way. But her soul did. That much was obvious in the way her breath hitched, in the way her pupils widened. The way she looked at me like I was a problem she wanted to solve and fuck in equal measure.

She thought she could hide in the library.

But I blocked the hall.

Let her get close enough to feel the tension between us. Close enough to breathe me in—to let her taste the promise of ruin. I didn't have to say much. Just one line, low and laced with enough French to haunt her later and give her a piece of me.

"You deserve better than this circus, *ma colombe*."

I left before I could push further. Because it wasn't time. Not yet.

But her reaction was everything I needed. Not fear. Not rejection.

Curiosity and that delicate fucking tremble she tried to hide.

That was the moment she knew it too—that her soul had already bent toward mine, and there was no turning back.

He's sloppy. Of course he is.

Men like Carson Gardner, born into power and licked into shape by money and legacy, always think they're invincible. They fuck what they want, snort what they want, buy their way out of trouble when it crawls a little too close to their designer shoes.

But me?

I *am* the trouble.

And I don't crawl. I gut.

I've imagined it. How I'll end him.

It won't be fast. Won't be clean. I'll strip the skin from his fingers first—make him watch each joint turn to raw pulp before I move on to the next. Break his knees so he can't run. Break his jaw so he can't beg. Then I'll cut off that smug fucking smile, piece by bleeding piece, until even his mother wouldn't recognize what's left.

And when he finally understands who I am—*what* I am—I'll whisper her name in his ear, just once, so he knows exactly why he's dying.

For her—always for her.

The club I follow him into smells like sweat and sin, tucked behind a boutique gym in a part of town that pretends to be upscale. The air is thick with heat and pheromones, the kind that stick to your skin long after you've left.

Music pulses through the walls—electronic, relentless—like it's trying to erase thought. Flashing lights strobe over too-thin bodies and vacant eyes, a pantomime of pleasure built on coercion. The stench is layered—spilled liquor, old bleach, desperation, fear masked in vanilla body spray.

It reminds me of a job I took in Prague—years ago now. A politician's son ran a similar den under the guise of a wellness lounge. Girls were trafficked in under fake modeling contracts. I broke both his legs before I slit his throat. He bled out screaming about diplomatic immunity.

Carson isn't so different. Same grin. Same god complex. Same certainty that the world bends for him.

And every step I take through this place, every breath I inhale, makes me want to put a bullet between his eyes now. But I don't. Because death, when done right, is an art. And art requires patience.

Carson goes straight to the back when I slip through the side entrance. They didn't need to ask for his name. The idiot announced himself to the bouncer like a celebrity. Waved his Rolex in the air and winked at the barely-legal redhead on his arm. She's nervous. She should be.

He definitely has a type. And it's not just "young."

It's *controlled*.

I set up in the surveillance room—a bribe and a threat got me access earlier today. Now it's just me, a bank of monitors, and a live feed into the worst corners of this city's underbelly. I watch him press a packet of powder into the girl's hand.

She hesitates.

He doesn't.

"*Tu vois ça?*" I mutter, angling the lens tighter as he grabs her chin.

You see that, ma colombe?

This is the man your father thought deserved you.

This is the bastard I'm supposed to approve.

He drags the redhead by the wrist into a champagne room. The door clicks shut.

I don't need to hear or see what happens next to know.

I've seen it too many times. Hell, I've cleaned up after it.

The girl stumbles out first, mascara streaking her cheeks—eyes dead. No one notices. No one helps.

He follows a few minutes later, grinning like he's done something worth smiling about.

I clench my fist, jaw tight.

By the time I've copied the full security footage, Carson's future is already circling the drain. This isn't just some sleazy night out—it's a map of his entire criminal network. Human trafficking, drug pipelines tied to rival syndicates, and bribes funneled through offshore accounts that connect straight to the enemies of Savannah's father.

Evidence, leverage, justification. And a nice little cherry on top.

***

BUT THE REAL OBSESSION—THE reason I haven't already put a bullet between Carson's eyes—is Savannah.

He will die. Make no mistake. I'll rip his throat out—for her, if for no other reason. But first, I need her to understand. What he is. What I am. And what it means to belong to a man like me.

I've been watching her, too. Closer than she could ever imagine.

In the mornings, she walks the rose garden alone. Always counterclockwise, always three full laps. A ritual carved from routine. Her hands trail along the blooms like they might anchor her. She never picks one. She never smiles.

It's not peace she's looking for. It's escape.

In the afternoons, she disappears into the music room. One no one else uses. It's off the main floor and out of the security camera lines of sight. I installed one, hidden behind the air vent.

And it's there I see her cradle the cello between her knees, her posture perfect but haunted. She plays pieces no one her age should know—Saint-Saëns, Fauré, Mahler. Melancholy compositions full of grief and ache. Music that sounds like bruises forming under skin. Every bow stroke is precise, but never mechanical. There's rage in her hands. Pain in her wrists. A kind of reverent violence she channels into every low-pitched note.

Sometimes, I close my eyes and imagine it differently. She's playing in my lap, back against my chest, breath stuttering as I ghost my fingers over the strings with her. Her legs are bare. Her pulse unsteady. Her music becomes something else—an offering, raw and fragile.

She never plays like this for anyone else. Only when she thinks no one is watching. When her walls drop and she lets the music speak truths she'd never dare say aloud.

Just herself. And now, for me.

And at night?

At night, she breaks my fucking heart.

And I didn't even know I had one until her.

She sleeps in silk. Always white. Always loose. Her windows almost always open to the night air, her door rarely locked. Not because she's naive. No—because she's already surrendered to the idea that no one will protect her. That no one *sees* her. That no one gives a fuck if she lives or dies.

I know that look. I've seen it in brothels where the girls don't ask for names. In war zones where innocence is a liability. In morgues where the corpses tell quieter truths than the living ever could.

So I become the shadow she doesn't see.

While they were at some fancy dinner, I mapped her entire suite. Cameras in the vents. Motion sensors behind the molding. Audio feed rigged into the thermostat.

I've memorized her body the way most men memorize blueprints. I know the delicate slope of her spine as she peels off her dress. The swell of her breasts when she stretches. The hollow behind her knee where she presses her fingers when she thinks too long.

I've watched her step out of the shower, steam curling around her like a lover who doesn't deserve her. Water runs down her chest in thin rivulets, trails over the soft curve of her belly, and clings to the shadow between her legs.

Her mouth parts like she's about to confess something to the mirror—but all that comes out is a breath. A curse. Maybe both.

She stares at her reflection like she hates it. Like she's daring it to strike first. Her hands grip the sink, knuckles pale, spine arched just enough to bare everything she pretends isn't breaking. And I swear—she's begging someone to fucking look.

I do.

I know when she turns over in bed. When she kicks off the sheet. When the panic starts in her chest and spirals down until her whole body is taut with ghosts she can't exorcise.

And I know what she does to forget.

I've watched her fingers disappear beneath black lace and white silk. Watched her hips rock as she fucks her own hand, breath catching in her throat like a prayer that doesn't know who it's meant for. Her other hand curls around one perfect breast, thumb teasing her nipple until she's panting—needy, pathetic, soaked. She bites her lip like she wants it rougher. Like she's picturing someone tearing the panties off instead of sneaking past the fabric.

She moans sometimes. But it's not enough.

It's not for Carson—I know that much.

I memorize it all.

And I start leaving her gifts.

A single white rose on her pillow. Pristine. Deliberate. Unmistakable. I watch from the monitor as she finds it—her fingers hovering over the bloom like it might vanish if she breathes too hard. She doesn't smile. Doesn't scream. She just stares, eyes wide, like a wire's been tripped somewhere deep inside her.

The next night, a bottle of her favorite wine—still sealed, but perfectly chilled. Her hand trembles when she lifts it from the silver tray I left it on. She smells the cork, sets it down without sipping. But she doesn't throw it away. Not even the note beneath it:

For the nights they try to make you forget who you are.

Then a strand of vintage pearls. The kind she'd said once, in a vapid bridal interview, made her feel timeless. Like her mother. I want her guessing. Want her hungry. I want her haunted by me in every mirror.

She hasn't worn them. But she didn't throw them away either. She tucked them into a drawer. Bottom right. Beneath her silks.

She doesn't know who leaves them. But she knows someone sees her. Really sees her.

I don't touch her.

Not yet.

But one night, the room is too quiet.

Too still.

There's a heaviness to the air. Something manufactured. Muted.

Sleeping pills. Probably ones Carson gave her—maybe even insisted on. Not enough to hurt her, just enough to keep her quiet. Convenient for him. Damning for me.

He doesn't give her peace.

He gives her silence.

I wait. Just long enough to make sure she's asleep. That the pills have done their job. That the cameras I planted haven't picked up a single fucking soul for the last thirty minutes but her.

Then I move.

Six slow steps across the balcony tile. No rush. No sound. My boots barely kiss the ground. I slide the door open—just enough to slip in sideways, silent as breath. Curtains shift like ghosts at my back.

The room smells like her. Like lavender and skin and something darker. Warmth clings to the air, thick and still. Every shadow obeys me here. Every inch of this space has been claimed. Tracked. Memorized.

And now, so will she.

She's sprawled on her side. One arm curled beneath her head. The sheet tangled low around her hips. Her cami has ridden up just enough to bare the soft curve of her back, the hint of her ribs, the slope of her ass. I lift the sheet slowly, carefully, until it's pooled at the backs of her knees.

She doesn't stir. Not even when I brush the edge of her cami higher. Not to touch. Just to see. To know. To take in every breath and line and delicate twitch of sleep that makes her real.

I lean closer, just above her skin. Not quite touching. I could count her freckles from here. Could mark them. Map them. Memorize them like I already fucking have.

She smells like heat and sleep and sin not yet committed. I nudge her legs apart, slow and reverent, like I'm parting scripture. Her skin is warm where the sheets had cocooned her, thigh pressed to thigh, heat radiating like an invitation.

I lean in, just close enough to inhale her cunt—ripe, sticky, the kind of scent that lives in a man's nostrils with obsession. Sweet and musky and utterly fucking obscene.

My hands tighten at my sides.

My cock twitches. I ignore it. And I don't touch her—not the way I want to.

This isn't the moment for that. This is the moment *before* that.

I kneel beside her bed and just breathe her in.

Lavender. Faint perfume. And something uniquely, maddeningly her.

She doesn't stir. Doesn't blink. Doesn't even dream, not really. She's too deep under.

So I lean in. Just enough to let my breath warm the curve of her cheek. My lips close to her ear. Voice barely a whisper.

"You'll be mine before the veil touches your skin."

It's not a threat.

It's a promise.

One I fully intend to keep.

Before I go, I scan the room one last time—and find them. Pale pink. Cotton. Discarded carelessly on the bathroom floor from before her shower, the gusset still soaked through with the scent of her. I pick them up slowly, reverently. Press them to my face and breathe in deep.

They smell like her cunt. Like lust and something that doesn't belong to me yet—but will. I close my eyes and hold the scent in my lungs until it burns.

Then I pocket them and slip out the way I came.

I disappear, back through the balcony door, before the night can betray me.

But even as I vanish, I know—

The hunt is nearly over.

And the claiming is about to begin.

4

COLD FEET

SAVANNAH

There's a white rose on my pillow.

Fresh. Dew-kissed. Pristine.

I sit up slowly, my pulse stuttering in the early morning hush. Carson wasn't at my house—he left yesterday for some final pre-wedding meeting with my father. I remember drifting off clearly. A glass of red wine. Half a Xanax to silence the screaming inside my skull. Silence, then sleep.

But this?

I reach for the rose like it might burn me. Fingertips brush the outermost petal, and it's still damp, like it was cut this morning. A thick green stem, no thorns. It smells faintly like rain and soap and something heady underneath the smell of the rose—something male.

I press it to my nose again, slower this time. There's a note of aftershave. Expensive. Earthy. Clean. Almost... familiar.

My thighs clench without permission.

It's ridiculous. I know it is. I'm not the kind of girl who romanticizes mystery suitors or fairy tale gestures. But this feels different—like a message tucked in silence. A whisper just for me.

I look around the room. Curtains untouched. The windows aren't open any wider than I left them. No sign of intrusion, no footprints on the carpet, I didn't hear the soft click of a lock disengaging in the night. But I feel it anyway.

Someone was here.

Someone *watched* me.

And not the way Carson looks at me when he's high and trying to fake affection for a woman he doesn't even like.

No.

This feels like obsession.

Like hunger.

I have this sixth sense telling me I've been seen in my sleep and *wanted.*

The part of me that should scream lies still and curious.

***

It HAPPENS AGAIN THE next night.

This time, it's a bottle of wine—vintage, French, older than I am—resting on the nightstand beside a single crystal glass and a note written in crimson ink so rich it could be blood:

For the nights they try to make you forget who you are.

The script is elegant, slanted, almost intimate. Like a secret whispered across silk sheets.

My throat goes tight. My fingertips tremble.

The bottle gleams in the dim light, a deep garnet hue catching the shadows like it knows a thousand sins and wants to spill them all down my throat. The glass beside it is etched with fine, curling details—old, expensive. Deliberate.

Carson didn't leave this. He only drinks bourbon, always neat—and he isn't even allowed in my bedroom, let alone sentimental enough to sneak in and leave me something beautiful. He wouldn't care enough to try.

He wouldn't think I needed remembering—wouldn't know I've been unraveling.

But someone does.

This... this feels like a dare. A promise. A reminder.

Not of who I'm expected to be.

But of who I *want* to be.

And maybe... who I could become if I let go.

***

THE PEARL NECKLACE COMES on the third night.

A thin velvet box placed on top of my pillow like an invitation—or a claim. No note this time, no instructions, just a strand of creamy, flawless pearls nestled in black velvet. Coiled like a secret. Like a collar.

My fingers tremble as I lift the strand. Cool against my skin, but somehow it burns. The silk cord slides over my knuckles, each pearl a drumbeat in my pulse. Heat blooms low, shame curling in its shadow, but I can't make myself put them down.

They shimmer under the soft glow of my bedside lamp, gleaming with a quiet elegance that dares me to wear them. To be owned. To be *seen*.

I touch them like they might vanish if I breathe too hard, fingers trembling as they ghost over the satiny surface.

My heart pounds so loud I wonder if he can hear it, wherever he is. If he's watching again. If he's close enough to see the pulse in my throat.

Because I know now.

It's him.

The man from the garden party—the one with the French accent that curled down my spine. The one whose ice-blue eyes made my stomach clench and my knees soften like they forgot how to hold me upright. The man hasn't left my mind since. He now lives in my blood. He crawls into my dreams with breath and heat and promises I shouldn't crave—but do.

God help me, I do.

***

I've started dreaming of him every night. Not just fleeting moments, not the kind of dreams that vanish in the morning mist. These are vivid, sensual—wrong.

It's never really his face I see—just the presence of him. The weight of heat curling at my spine. A breath against the back of my neck, slow and deliberate, like he knows exactly what he's doing to me. The ghost of a hand dragging over my ribs, fingers resting possessively on the curve of my hip.

Last night, I swear I moaned into my pillow.

I woke soaked—panties drenched, thighs slick, nipples tight and aching beneath the thin veil of my camisole. My entire body hummed with need. With memory. With something too dark to name.

And the worst part?

It didn't feel like a violation.

It felt like a fucking *claim*.

I felt branded. Possessed. Worshipped.

I could still feel the phantom imprint of his mouth behind my ear—the rasp of stubble, the molten heat of breath as he whispered into my skin: *mine*.

And I wasn't afraid.

I was seen. Claimed so completely it makes shame curl down my spine and settle molten-hot in my gut.

God help me, I think I felt loved.

Even now, in the cruel honesty of daylight, I feel him under my skin—an echo pulsing low and deep, like the ghost of a bruise I don't want to heal.

He's in the softest parts of me. In my fucking *dreams*.

And I don't even know his name.

I've thought about asking. Daddy, maybe. Or one of the security detail who always lingers just a little too long. Someone has to know. Men like him don't just appear. Someone let him in. Vetted him. Positioned him.

He must have belonged at that party. But he also stood there like he *owned* it.

And he looked at me like I already belonged to him.

Now he's haunting me.

And I can't stop wondering what he'd say if I found him and asked him to never let me go.

***

I FIND HER IN the garden—my best friend and maid of honor, Madeline. The only person in my world who feels real. But even she plays by the rules, believes in the system. Trains for her future like it's a privilege and not a sentence. She still thinks our last names mean something worth protecting.

She's barefoot on the stone bench under the trellis, toes painted the same shade of pale pink as the roses overhead. The sun is just beginning to dip, painting the horizon in soft amber. There are no staff nearby. No security pretending not to listen.

That's why I invited her here.

Because I need to say it out loud.

She lifts her head when I approach, eyes narrowing the way they always do when she senses something's off. "You look like you saw a ghost."

"Worse," I say, folding onto the bench beside her. My voice is quieter than I intend. "I think I've been dreaming about someone who's real."

Madeline blinks. "What does that mean?"

I tell her everything.

The gifts. The scent of him on my pillow. The dreams that feel more like memories. The ache between my thighs when I wake. The feeling of being *watched.*

"Savannah," she says, her voice flat with disbelief. "You realize how fucked up that sounds, right? If someone's been in your room—if they've been touching your things—you should be calling the cops, not... *getting wet* over it."

"He hasn't hurt me."

"Yet," she snaps. "Jesus, Savannah. That's not the point. You have a fiancé. A future. You're a Hale, for God's sake. And you're sitting here talking about mystery stalkers like you're in some sick bodice-ripper."

"You don't get it," I whisper. "I feel safer with him in the shadows than I do with Carson in broad daylight."

Her expression goes cold. "Carson is your fiancé. He's your duty. Our families—"

"—don't care if he cheats or hurts me when he's high," I hiss. "They care about optics. But *this man*? He sees me. He leaves me things I didn't even know I wanted. And when I dream of him, it's the only time I feel *alive.*"

Madeline recoils, arms crossed tight across her chest. "You sound insane. You *sound* like a girl asking to be kidnapped."

"Maybe I am," I say quietly. "Maybe I want someone to take me away from all of this. Someone who looks at me like I'm not just a pawn in their fucking game."

Madeline stares at me like she's seeing a stranger. "You don't even know his name."

"No," I admit. "But I know the way he makes me feel. And it's more honest than anything Carson or any other man has ever given me."

Her mouth tightens into a flat line. "I'm going to ask around. And if I find anything—*anything*—you're going to listen to me. No excuses. No fantasy."

I nod. Even though I know I won't.

Because every night I close my eyes, he's there. And a part of me—maybe the broken and twisted part—*wants* him to be.

***

I DIDN'T SEE HER the next day. Or the one after that. By the end of the week, it was like she'd been erased—her absence was another silent message I wasn't brave enough to read.

At first, I told myself she was busy. She was always busy—etiquette classes, legacy dinners she couldn't skip. But she always found time for me. Always. And this time, she was supposed to meet me for my final dress fitting. My last chance to stand in front of a mirror and pretend this was still a dream I might actually want.

But she never showed. Never called. Never even sent a text.

By the second day after, her phone goes straight to voicemail. By the third, her mother is frantic—calling everyone, claiming she left a note and went to clear her head, that she just needed a break before the wedding chaos. But no one's seen her. No one's heard from her. And deep down, I know she didn't leave on her own.

Madeline would've told me.

I know she would've.

She wasn't scared. She was livid—because of what I told her in the garden. Because I said I *liked* what he was doing to me. Because I told her I felt safer in the shadows with a stranger than in broad daylight with my fiancé. Because I dared to speak of wanting more than duty and legacy and a name that meant nothing to me anymore.

She was *disgusted* by me, by what I was feeling, by the way I spoke of this man like he wasn't a monster. Like I wanted him. Her eyes didn't dart—they blazed. She was going to dig until she unearthed him, drag him into the light, and destroy whatever spell he'd cast over me.

And now she's gone.

No goodbye. No warning. No trace.

Until an envelope appears.

No return address. No signature. Just a small square of heavy paper tucked beneath my vanity mirror that wasn't there the night before.

The handwriting matches the others. That same elegant, slanted script that looks almost too intimate to be cruel:

Your friend was digging too deep. She doesn't respect what we are to one another. Don't worry, ma colombe. She's not a problem anymore.

My stomach twists and my knees buckle.

I stare at the words until they blur, rereading them again and again. My hands tremble. My throat locks up.

He doesn't mean she's dead—he can't, not really.

Right?

Except then the second note appears in the same place that night.

Ivory parchment. A single line in the same crimson ink:

Say "I do" and I'll kill him at the altar.

I should scream. Should run to my father.

But I don't.

Because the most terrifying part isn't the threat.

It's the thrill.

Somehow, I'm not horrified that he might've hurt Madeline—or that he's threatening Carson.

I'm horrified that I'm *not* horrified.

That something inside me—something dark and wicked and full of feminine rage and submission all at once—*likes* knowing he'd remove obstacles. *For me.*

That someone in this world is watching every step I take, tracing my shadow like a vow, whispering *mine* with every breath I draw.

And worse... that I want him to. That the sound of that possessive promise coils around my spine like silk and steel. That it doesn't scare me—it soothes me.

It stains me with want.

Has my life really been this fucked up?

That this—the threat of violence wrapped in obsession—feels like the safest offer I've ever had? That a man who wants to slit my fiancé's throat, who might've killed my best friend, feels like a *better* option than anyone this world or my family has ever handed me?

Maybe Madeline was never really *my* best friend.

Maybe she was just the best friend my mother chose for me. Groomed for appearances. Loyal to the name, not the girl behind it. Polite, pretty, and perfectly aligned with the life I was supposed to want.

And now that she's gone... I can't tell if I miss her—or just the idea of her.

The truth is, I don't think I've ever had a *real* friend. Not someone who saw *me*. Not someone who would've stayed if I told them the darkest parts of who I am, what I want.

But *he* sees me.

What does all of that say about me?

What does all of that say about *them*?

5

UNINVITED

LEON

IT'S ALMOST POETIC, REALLY. The calm before the carnage.

Savannah is sleeping in silk tonight. Somewhere across this cursed city, she's dreaming under the weight of a wedding veil someone else chose. And this bastard? Carson Gardner? He's sipping bourbon in a suite he didn't earn, dicking around before he dons a tuxedo he doesn't deserve.

He has no idea what's coming.

But I do.

I've been dreaming of this.

I bypass the door like it's nothing. Security code, cameras, alarms—they're for amateurs. Her father gave me access, but I stepped in the room on my own. I'm a whisper in the dark. A ghost with a blade.

The suite is quiet, lit by the dull amber glow of expensive lighting and entitlement. He's sprawled on the couch, tie undone, sleeves rolled up, ego swollen—the picture of smug filth the night before he's meant to marry the most precious fucking creature on this planet.

And he has a half-naked girl in his bed. Some doped-up teenage substitute with smeared lipstick and vacant eyes. Barely legal, barely conscious. I can smell the vodka from here.

Fucking predictable.

I move fast.

The girl hits the floor first—soft, safe, out cold. I cradle her head, just for a moment, and set her beside the couch. She won't remember this. That's a mercy I've reserved for her. She might not think so when she wakes to my work of art.

He tries to stand.

Too late.

My boot slams into his chest, pinning him back.

He chokes, flailing like a caught fish.

"You—what the fuck—"

That's all he gets out before the syringe finds his throat.

Something slow. Something painful.

I don't give him the gift of unconsciousness.

"*Bonjour, connard*," I murmur, tilting my head. "You know who I am?"

He blinks, dazed, groaning as the drug melts through him. I let the silence stretch. Just long enough for his heart to start pounding. Just long enough for him to wonder why his skin feels like it's boiling.

"I'm your reaper. I'm the man your fiancée deserves. And you—you're the last mistake her family will ever make for her."

I strip my gloves off, finger by finger, and lay them out with the same reverence I might reserve for laying silver at a feast. Each movement is slow, precise. Then I roll up my sleeves. A ritual. A purge.

"You're not dying fast, Gardner. Not tonight. Tonight, you give me everything."

I start with the fingers.

The cigar cutter is an elegant thing. Polished chrome. Perfect weight. Satisfying click.

I line it up with his pinky. Just below the first knuckle.

Click.

He shrieks like a kicked dog, his back arching off the floor. Blood spurts in a fine mist, dotting my arms.

"That's for the girl I found in your bed," I whisper.

Click.

The ring finger next. He's begging now, choking on spit and blood and panic.

"Please, please—I didn't touch Savannah—I swear to God—"

I lean in, voice low. "I know, and I'm fucking glad you pretended to care about her virtue."

Click.

Middle finger. That one takes more effort. Cartilage resists. I twist the cutter slightly to finish the job. He screams until his throat goes hoarse.

By the fourth, he's confessing.

The truth spills out in wet gasps—names of girls. Ages. The offshore accounts. Hidden cameras. Money funneled through charities. A fucking empire built on stolen innocence.

It's worse than I thought.

But that's good.

Because I'm worse, too.

I drag a blade down his chest. Shallow, deliberate.

I paint the suite in ribbons of red. It spatters across the cream sofa, splashes up the gold-threaded curtains. Arcs in a sickeningly beautiful spray across the mirrored bar and drips in slow, lazy streaks down the edge of the coffee table. His blood seeps into the rug beneath us—some imported antique worth more than most people's cars—and crawls toward the velvet ottoman like it wants to stain everything he touched. Even the walls get a taste. I want Savannah to see this room and feel the aftermath in her bones.

The ruin I made for her.

The offering.

The art.

"*Tu veux voir ce que je fais aux hommes qui regardent ma colombe?*" I hiss, slicing lower.

He sobs. Blubbers.

"You're fucking insane—she's my—"

Wrong answer.

I press the heel of my boot against his shattered hand and crush it until he pukes."She was never yours. You were just the parasite they pinned to her like a corsage."

I press record on a burner phone. Angle it so the camera catches every ruinous inch of him—bloodied, blubbering, broken. I want her to see what I see. I want her to feel it.

"Talk. To her. Now."

He gurgles, shaking his head like he still thinks he has a choice.

So I break his jaw and hear the satisfying crack. Then I hand him a towel to catch the blood spilling from his face like guilt finally finding a voice.

"Talk, Carson. Tell her what you did. Tell her why she'll never have to see your face again."

He sobs into the camera. Tries to string together words through cracked teeth and coagulated shame. Slurred confessions. Names. Details. The underage girls. The drugs. The buyers. The way he planned to steal her daddy's money.

And every time he pauses too long, I remind him with the knife. Pressed just enough against skin to make him remember what pain tastes like.

I don't speak. I let him confess. Let him give her every ounce of the filth he buried beneath cufflinks and cocaine.

Because this isn't just a kill.

It's a gift.

And she needs to know exactly what I've removed from her life. Exactly what I've replaced.

When I'm done, I let him lie there. Gutted. Gasping.

Then I kneel. Low. Close. So close I can see the whites of his eyes flood with capillaries. Let him see mine. Let him know who sends him to hell.

"She'll never think of you again."

I drag the blade across his throat—slow, angled, a brutal kiss of steel through skin, sinew, and muscle. I don't rush it. I *savor* it.

Not clean. Not quick.

I *paint* with his blood again.

The first spurt of blood hits my cheek like a blessing. The second sprays across the hardwood in a wild arc, slapping against the baseboards and staining the hem of the curtain. Thick streams pulse from the gash, coating my hands, his chest, the floor between us. It fills his mouth, bubbles from his nose. He twitches, gasps, claws weakly at the air as if death might offer a hand back.

It doesn't.

His eyes roll. His bowels release. Fucking gross. The final indignity—his body voiding itself like the sack of waste he is. I wrinkle my nose but don't move. Let the stench hang heavy in the air. Let it mark the room with the truth of who he was.

Blood pools beneath him, black in the dim light.

I wrap her wedding veil around my hand, then dip it in his blood like it's being baptized.

She'll understand the message.

She was never meant to walk that aisle.

Not with him.

I leave the burner phone still recording, propped against the blood-soaked couch cushion. Let whoever finds this room hear the truth echoing in the background.

Then I scatter the rest—the files, the flash drive, the photos. I tear open the hidden compartments in the ottoman. Leave the cash out in piles. A trail of rot and receipts.

Everything Carson was. Everything he did. Laid bare like an autopsy.

And when I turn toward the girl—still unconscious, curled like a broken doll on the rug—I let myself pause.

She'll wake to hell. To blood. To violence. To freedom.

One last glance. One second of quiet.

Then I vanish like smoke.

6

SOMETHING RED

SAVANNAH

THE BOX IS SMALL.

Too small for a dress. Too light for shoes. And yet, it feels heavy in my hands—like it's holding its breath.

I don't know what I expected when the parcel was dropped at my door. No signature. No knock. Just a silent arrival, as if fate itself had crept down the hall and left it there like a curse. The staff didn't mention it. No one even seemed to notice it—but the second my fingers brushed the smooth wrapping, my pulse began to riot. My palms dampened. It felt like the box knew it wasn't welcome here.

White satin paper, wrapped with military precision.

A single ribbon—blood red, pulled so tight it bites into the edges.

No card. No tag. No gentle clue to soften what's waiting for me inside. Just the quiet, smirking hum of inevitability winding up my spine as I untie the ribbon and lift the lid.

The smell hits before I see anything.

Copper. Carnal. A dark, metallic tang that feels like it coats my teeth just breathing it in.

Then I see it.

My veil. The one I was supposed to wear today.

It's drenched.

Soaked from tip to comb, the delicate lace bloated and stiff with congealed, drying blood. It clings to itself in sticky folds, threads matted and stained a deep, unforgiving crimson.

The scream tears out of me without warning—raw, jagged, feral. It shreds my throat as the box slips from my grip, crashing to the marble. The veil spills out like an omen, pooling in a wet, macabre sprawl that looks too much like a scalped head.

Because it is.

Not literally, I pray.

But in spirit?

He sent me a headless wedding.

There's a note tucked beneath the tissue and plastic. Heavy stock, expensive—meant for elegant invitations and society announcements. Instead, one sentence bleeds across it in thick red strokes.

No. Not strokes—stains. Browned at the edges.

It's blood.

You're free now, little dove.

I fold. Not just around the paper—around myself. My knees hit the floor, veil whispering against my skin, cold and damp.

The scream must carry, because within seconds I hear footsteps pounding up the stairs, my father's sharp voice cutting through the chaos. Doors open, voices rise—the household already buzzing with preparations for the garden wedding below now tilts into panic.

I can't move as they pour into the hallway and then my room. My father freezes when he sees the veil. Someone gasps. Another swears under their breath. Then everything blurs—phones come out, calls are made, orders barked. By the time law enforcement arrives, the room smells of blood and expensive perfume, laced with the bitter tang of fear.

I think I already knew, but now we all know—once the investigators begin talking among themselves. I can't hear all of their words, but I can see it in the way their eyes shift toward me, the way their shoulders tense. Something terrible waits in whatever they've found.

Then they tell us of evidence left behind in Carson's hotel suite, confessions captured on video, every sin laid bare for them, but not yet for me.

My father's expression hardens as he listens to the officers.

He doesn't ask who could have done it. He already knows—but he doesn't say anything until the police have left.

When my father gives a voice to the name, it hits me like a pulse under the skin—Leon. He hired him to dig for dirt, not to spill blood. But the set of his jaw says he's already plotting his next move.

He's trying to find Leon Mercier—the man who has been my shadow, the one who has haunted my dreams and breathed life into my nightmares.

That weight that used to crush my chest? Gone.

In its place is something sharp. Something electric.

Something alive.

Carson is dead.

And I should be broken. Horrified. Shaking apart—at least, that's what my mother and the rest of the family seem to expect as they gather around me, murmuring comfort I don't need or want.

But I'm not.

I'm free.

He killed for me.

No. Not for me.

Because of me.

Because he wanted me.

And God help me, I want to know what that kind of devotion feels like pressed into my skin.

✳✳✳

THEY MOVE ME TO a luxury hotel suite by nightfall—my father muttering something about keeping me "safe," though we both know it's also to keep the press at bay. I let them fuss, let my mother choose my clothes for dinner as if the act can stitch the day back together. We sit in the restaurant downstairs, the three of us, pretending to eat while their eyes keep darting to the lobby, to the doors, to each other.

By the time I return upstairs, the hallway feels too quiet. The key card is cold in my hand. I push the door open, expecting empty, sterile calm.

Instead, he's there.

Leon.

Just waiting.

I know I should scream. I should back away, run and pound on my parents' door, race to the security stationed at the elevator. I should remember that if I step into that room that I'll be alone with him.

But I also realize he is giving me that choice. He could have stayed hidden, but he didn't. He's presenting himself to me.

It's an offer—it's the choice to consent.

Every logical part of me screams to back away. Instead, my instincts and my feet carry me toward him, the copper tang of phantom blood mixing with the scent of his cologne until it's all I can taste.

While it should be fear, something else floods me—hot and low, curling deep in my core. The same electric awareness I felt in those dreams I kept trying to tell myself were nightmares. The same breathless pull that makes me grateful, in some terrible and selfish way, that I'll never have to marry Carson.

His eyes pin me in place, dark and certain. And the worst—or maybe best—part? I don't want to be anywhere else.

I step inside. Without breaking eye contact, I close the door behind me and turn the deadbolt. It's not spoken, but it's consent all the same.

His mouth curves—danger and possession in one slow, lethal smile. "*J'ai peint les murs avec son sang, ma colombe.* Now I want to mark you the same way."

He starts toward me slowly, each step deliberate, a predator closing the last inches to its prey. His pace gives me time to object or retreat. There's a quiet poetry in the way he moves—like he's crossing a threshold no one else can see, like the room bends around his will. He stops a breath away, heat licking over my skin.

"*Est-ce que tu as peur de moi?*" His voice is a knife wrapped in velvet and I'm grateful for the three years of French I was forced to take—I don't understand everything he says, but I understood that one. *Are you afraid of me?*

I should be. I should scream. I should run. I should remember the blood and the veil and the way my life just ended and began this morning. I should be the girl they raised—polite, obedient, afraid.

"I know I should be," I whisper, truth cracking open in my chest. "But I'm not."

Something dark and bright flickers in his eyes—relief, ruin. It's too much, I look away.

"*Regarde-moi,*" he says as a soft command. *Look at me.*

His hand slides into my hair, drawing me to him, and his mouth claims mine.

The first rush is heat and pressure, his lips hard and certain against mine, tasting faintly of coffee and something darker—metallic and copper, like the echo of what he's done.

His scent wraps around me—clean soap over gun oil, leather, and the faintest trace of blood. My pulse stutters, then pounds, every nerve sparking as his stubble scrapes my skin and his breath mingles with mine. I can feel the slow drag of his mouth, the deliberate sweep of his tongue against my lower lip before he deepens the kiss, coaxing me open until the world tilts and I am drowning in him—violence and sweetness braided together, burning away the last fragments of the girl I was this morning.

His hands are on me before I can think, sliding down my spine, gripping my hips like he's anchoring me in place. The kiss turns hungrier, more demanding, and my body answers before my mind can form the words. When his palms skim the curve of my thighs, I willingly hook my legs around his waist, offering myself to his hold as he lifts me, my gasp spilling into his mouth—not in fear but in raw anticipation.

And then I feel it—hard, thick, unmistakable—pressing against the tender heat at my core. The contact sends a shockwave through me, my body instinctively grinding closer, chasing more of that pressure. Heat coils low in my belly, sharp and liquid all at once, and I can't stop the small, needy sound that escapes me. The friction is maddening, a silent promise of what's coming, and I don't want it to stop.

The sound makes him still for a heartbeat, his gaze dropping to mine. "You've never been touched like this, have you?" It's not really a question—it's a verdict.

I shake my head, breathless. "No."

Something primal ignites behind his eyes. His thumb drags along my lower lip, smearing the moisture there as if he's already marking me. "*Mon ange déchu...* my fallen angel," he murmurs, almost reverent. "I get to be the first. The only."

The way he says it—like a vow, like a sentence—makes the ache between my thighs almost unbearable. I should be terrified of what that means, but all I feel is claimed, chosen, wanted in a way that obliterates doubt.

He carries me across the room as if I weigh nothing, his mouth devouring mine the whole way. The world spins until my back hits the bed, the mattress dipping beneath me. Before I can catch my breath, he's straightening, eyes raking over me like he's deciding which piece to unwrap first.

And then he's on me—hands at my dress, yanking, tearing fabric down my body with a ferocity that steals the air from my lungs. Every inch of newly bared skin feels fever-hot under his gaze, like I'm being stripped not just of clothes but of every shield I've ever worn.

When his hands reach the thin lace between my thighs, there's no hesitation—he hooks his fingers in and rips my panties apart with a single, brutal motion. The sound of tearing fabric snaps through the air, and my breath catches, my body clenching with the shock and thrill of it. I've never felt so exposed... or so wholly belonging to anyone else.

He pauses, eyes locked on mine. "Are you scared now?"

I shake my head slowly, heart pounding. "No."

Something in his expression sharpens—approval laced with hunger. Then he's lowering himself between my thighs, his hands spreading me open with deliberate, unyielding control. The first sweep of his tongue is hot and devastating, dragging through my slick skin like he owns every gasp that leaves me.

His mouth works in slow, claiming strokes, then faster, more ravenous, until I'm trembling under him. Fingers join the wet heat of his mouth, thrusting in time with the rhythm of his tongue, curling deep until I see white. The sounds—his low growl, the wet pull of his mouth, my own desperate moans—fill the room like a cacophony of sensuality.

I can't think, can't breathe, can't be anything but the girl being undone by him, claimed in the most primal way possible... and loving every second of it.

Pleasure tears through me in sharp, relentless waves, my body arching against his mouth as release crashes over me. I cry out, clutching at the sheets, every muscle shaking until I'm left gasping, dazed in the aftermath.

He rises slowly, his mouth glistening, eyes burning as he watches me come down from the high he gave me. Without a word, he strips—shirt first, then belt, then trousers—until he's bare before me.

I freeze. I've never seen a man naked in person, let alone aroused, and the sight of him is both breathtaking and intimidating. My gaze drags down his chest, over the taut lines of muscle, before landing on the thick length straining toward me. My breath hitches, heat pooling low again, but the words slip out before I can stop them. "There's no way that will go inside me."

The slow, dangerous smile that curves his lips says otherwise. "It will fit, little dove." He pauses and strokes himself while his bottom lip catches on his teeth. "You'll take every inch, and by the time I'm done, you'll beg me not to stop."

Then his mouth is back on my skin—hot, wet, relentless—trailing up my thigh, each kiss a brand, each scrape of teeth a warning and a promise. My muscles tighten with every inch he climbs, the heat of him searing into me as he reaches my belly. His tongue flicks and swirls against sensitive skin, and I gasp when his hands glide up to cup my breasts, thumbs rolling my nipples until they're peaked and aching. Every nerve in my body feels wired to him, pulled taut and trembling.

He takes my nipple into his mouth, sucking hard enough to make my toes curl, then releases it with a wet sound that makes me clench around nothing. His mouth drags up my sternum, over the fluttering pulse in my throat, until he's at my neck again—biting, licking, claiming.

Before I can even catch my breath, my wrists are pinned above my head in one of his hands. The other grips my hip in a bruising hold, keeping me exactly where he wants me. He looks me dead in the eye—dark, merciless, and beautiful—just before he surges forward, driving into me in one brutal, unrelenting stroke that brands every nerve with the truth of who he is.

It's fire and pleasure all at once—sharp enough to steal the air from my lungs, hot enough to melt every last thought from my head. I cry out, the sound caught somewhere between shock and need, my body stretching and clenching around him as he groans like he's been starving for this. The stretch is intense, almost too much, but the burn only fuels the molten ache building deep inside me.

He doesn't release my wrists and he doesn't look away. Not for a second. Every thrust is a vow, every slow grind a reminder that I'm his now, that he's inside me and there's no going back. And God help me—I don't want to.

After a few more deep, claiming thrusts, he pulls out abruptly, my body clenching around the loss. Before confusion can bloom, his hand slides between my thighs and two fingers push inside me, curling and stroking until my hips jerk up in pure instinct. His thumb presses against my clit while his fingers work me open, and I feel the unmistakable wet warmth slicking his touch.

He withdraws slowly, deliberately, holding my gaze as he lifts his hand into the light. My breath catches when I see the crimson and pink staining his fingers—my blood, vivid against his skin.

"Your virgin cunt just gave me its first gift," he murmurs, voice thick with reverence and sin. "And it's mine to keep."

Then he paints me with it—dragging those blood-slicked fingers over my hipbones, circling my nipples, tracing the hollow of my throat. The sensation is molten and obscene, the metallic scent of me mixing with his heat until I'm dizzy.

He dips back into me for more, fingers plunging deep to gather fresh crimson before smearing it across my skin like an artist layering a masterpiece. Again and again, he returns for more paint, even as the pink fades to clear, each stroke of his hand making my breath hitch and my thighs tremble. He brings his fingers to his mouth and sucks them, groaning low, before pressing them to my lips.

"Taste it, little dove. Taste what you've given me." The command is velvet and steel. My tongue darts out before I can think, licking the copper tang from his skin. It should be strange, wrong, but instead it makes my pulse thunder and my core clench with hungry need.

"No one else will ever be inside you," he whispers against my ear, voice like a dark hymn. "This blood binds us. Last night, I painted walls with a man's life. Tonight, I paint you—and you're the most beautiful masterpiece I'll ever create."

His eyes glitter as he asks, "Did you see the art I made for you last night?"

I shake my head, breathless. The corner of his mouth lifts before he reaches for a phone. A swipe, and the video plays—Carson's battered, blood-slick face filling the screen. His voice is broken, wet with pain, spilling every crime he's ever committed. My stomach flips when the camera pulls back, revealing the carnage Leon left of him.

And then his voice, low and certain, draws my attention back to him. "And Madeline? They'll never find her. I promise you, *ma colombe*... I protect what's mine."

I should be horrified. My pulse should spike with fear, my stomach should twist with revulsion. Instead, heat floods me. My skin electrifies; my body aches for him with a hunger that's wrong and thrilling all at once. I hate that I'm this far gone. Hate that the monster he is only makes me want him more.

Before I can process it all, his mouth is back on me, licking the trails of blood and arousal from my skin, his tongue slow and deliberate, before his cock plunges back inside me in one savage thrust. The rhythm he sets is brutal and consuming, each drive of his hips a demand, each withdrawal a taunt, until I'm trembling around him. The slick heat of the fluid between us only seems to drive him harder, and his mouth keeps finding more of me to taste.

I can't tell where pain ends and pleasure begins—it's all one devastating wave, crashing through me again and again. His teeth graze my throat, his growl vibrating into my bones as he fucks me harder, deeper, until the air leaves my lungs in ragged gasps.

He finally lets my wrists go to grip both my hips, slamming into me once, twice, and then with a guttural grunt, he spills inside me, his body shuddering with release.

My hands move with a mind of their own. One of them wraps around the thick muscles of his arm, the fingers of the other threading through his short, sweat-dampened hair.

He doesn't soften his hold, doesn't let me go—his lips are against my ear, his voice rough and wicked.

"Feel that, little dove? My seed is in you now, right where it belongs. I'll fill you until you can't take another drop, and you'll carry me inside you for days. Every time you move, you'll feel me—reminding you you're mine."

After a few moments, his touch shifts—still possessive, but slower.

He gathers me up against his chest, carrying me into the bathroom like I weigh nothing. Steam is practically curling in the air before he sets me on the counter, wiping my skin clean with a warm cloth. His hands are methodical, tender even, tracing over the marks he's left as though committing them to memory.

He lowers me into the hot bath, the water lapping at my skin. He kneels beside the tub, washing me himself, his fingers gentle now, gliding soap over my shoulders, my breasts, down my thighs. Every pass feels like he's both soothing me and branding me again, in a different way.

When he finishes, he cups my face, forcing my gaze to his.

"What are you going to do with me now?" I whisper.

His mouth curves into something dangerous and sure. "Keep you."

7

THE HONEYMOON

LEON

THE HOTEL SUITE STILL smells of sex and sin, the bed a wrecked monument to what we just did. I watch her move, slow and deliberate, gathering herself while the city hums beyond the windows.

"We can't stay here," I tell her, voice low but certain. "Too many eyes. Too many people who want to drag you back."

She meets my gaze without hesitation. "I know. Nobody would understand, but..." her voice softens, "I'd follow you anywhere."

Pressing a soft kiss to her forehead, I respond, "You are *ma princesse*. You'll never want for anything. I'll treat you like the princess you are to me."

Her lips part, the smallest smile touching them. "Leon," she says, in reverence but also as if she's testing the name in her mouth, claiming it.

She packs the few things she had in the suite. Then we leave, my hand firm on hers as we vanish into the night.

The drive is quiet until asphalt gives way to gravel, the kind of road you don't find unless you're meant to. Pines crowd the sky, their black needles clawing at the last sliver of daylight.

She's curled in the passenger seat, knees drawn up, wearing the dress I tore her out of hours ago. My jacket is around her shoulders. She doesn't thank me for it. But I don't give a fuck about her manners. I care that she's here—*mine.*

I can't keep my hands off her—her thigh, her hair, her hand. She welcomes every touch, leaning into each one like it's a tether.

She studies me like she's trying to map the monster who just burned her old life to ash. "Leon, tell me about you," she says finally, her voice too steady for a girl whose world just ended.

I laugh once, low and humorless. "Brutal honesty, *ma colombe?* You won't like it."

"I don't like being lied to."

Fair enough. "I'm thirty-eight," I tell her.

Her mouth tilts, eyes sparking. "*Technically* old enough to be my father."

I glance at her, let the corner of my mouth curl slowly. "*Non.* Old enough to be your man. The boys your family tried to sell you to? They'd never know what to do with you. They'd fuck you like porcelain—afraid to break you. Me?" My voice drops, rough and deliberate. "I'll ruin you until you don't even remember their names."

The flush that climbs up her neck is enough of a response for me. "I'm a dual citizen. Born in New Orleans, raised between there and Marseille. My father was an assassin for men richer than God. My mother—" I shake my head. "She didn't survive him."

She goes still, but I'm not done. "My trade is paid in blood—and far worse. Yet I hold more power and wealth than the family who tried to sell you to the devil."

Her lips curve, slow and knowing. "Some would say I walked into hell on my own, with a different devil."

I catch her hand, kiss each finger like a benediction and a claim all in one, lingering until I feel her shiver.

"I learned early in life that women are decorations. Distractions. Soft bodies to fuck when I wanted, discard when I didn't. I didn't think I could care about one. Didn't want to. Then..." My grip tightens on the wheel. "The day I saw you, *putain de merde*, I knew I was fucked."

Her breath catches.

"I have never been obsessed with a woman before you, Savannah. Never hunted one. Never planned to keep one. And now—" I glance at her, letting her see the wolf in the headlights. "*Ma colombe*, you breathe because I let you. And I breathe because you exist—and if you ever stopped, so would I."

Her brows lift. "Was that at the garden party?"

"*Non.*" My mouth curves without humor. "When I was running surveillance on Carson. I watched you, your eyes dead, and I thought—*non*, that won't do."

She swallows. "And now?"

I let the corner of my mouth lift, slow and feral. "Ever since I painted you with blood, I've never seen your eyes more alive."

***

THE CABIN'S SHADOW APPEARS through the trees, a black shape on the mountainside. Remote. Silent. A place no one will find her.

I kill the engine. "Welcome home."

Stepping out first, I scan the tree line before opening her door. My hand never leaves the small of her back as I lead her up the wide porch. The wood under our feet is solid, polished, not the creaking ruin people picture when they think "remote cabin."

Inside, her eyes go wide. Not fear—wonder. The space is modern and warm, stone fireplace and leather furniture, steel-and-glass kitchen gleaming under recessed lights.

"Completely off-grid," I tell her, shutting the door behind us. "Solar and generator power. Well water. Satellite internet in a dead man's name."

She laughs, soft and startled, like she can't believe she's doing this.

I guide her toward the long farmhouse table where my laptop already waits. I open the screen to a luxury retailer's site. "We start now. Clothes, lingerie, shoes, toiletries, whatever you want—fill the cart." I lean over her, my voice brushing her ear. "*Ma poupée.* All painted up, all mine."

Her brows lift. "Now?"

"*Oui, ma colombe.* Tonight." I drag the mouse slowly, making her watch each page load. "You'll want for nothing here. And tomorrow, we'll take a trip—buy you anything else you need. Anything you want. There is no limit for you."

I pull a small box from my coat and set it in front of her. She opens it to find a brand-new phone.

"You can even keep your social media," I say, brushing a lock of hair from her face. "But no pictures. At least not of me, not of you, not of the cabin. You can tell them you're safe. That you chose to leave."

Her thumb strokes the edge of the phone like it's a strange, delicate gift. "Chose to leave," she repeats, voice low, eyes still drinking in the place that's now both her freedom and her cage.

Her "chose to leave" hangs in the air between us, a vow she doesn't even realize she's made. I take it for what it is—consent to everything I want.

She's still holding the phone when I close the laptop, her pulse visible in the hollow of her throat. The fire catches in her eyes, flickering between fear and something close to excitement.

"I can't wait to taste you again," I murmur, voice thick with hunger.

Her lips part, a question trembling there, but I'm already taking the phone from her hand and setting it aside. My chair scrapes against the wood as I sit, slow and deliberate. Then I point to the table.

"Up."

She hesitates—just long enough for defiance to spark—then obeys. Barefoot, careful, she climbs onto the table until she's sitting where my plate would be. I drag her forward by the knees, parting them, and she gasps as the wood cools her thighs.

I hook her panties with one finger and drag them down her legs. They hit the floor with a soft sound. The scent of her is immediate—warm, sweet, trembling.

"Hands flat on the table," I say, voice low enough to be dangerous. "Let me see what's mine."

Her breath shudders as she obeys.

For a moment, I just look at her.

Dress hitched high.

Her pulse hammering like a trapped bird against her neck.

My hands slide up her calves, over her knees, until my thumbs press into the soft inside of her thighs. I spread her wider, slow, forcing her to feel every inch of exposure.

This time, I really take in the sight of her spread open for me—the most inviting, beautiful pink, hairless pussy I've ever seen. The kind of perfection that makes a man want to ruin it just to prove it's real.

I lean in, voice roughening. "This cunt belongs to me," I growl. "My cunt. You'll let me see it, taste it, fuck it whenever I want. Do you understand?"

Her breath catches, and after a heartbeat that feels a little too long, she whispers, "Yes."

"*Regarde moi*," I order.

When she does, I smirk. "Good girl."

Then I bow my head.

My tongue plunges into her slick heat, fucking her with it until she's shaking, a helpless sound spilling from her throat. I drag my mouth up to her clit and suck, filthy and hungry, until she arches like she's about to break. She's gripping the edge of the table, knuckles white, breath coming out in desperate little gasps that sound like my name. I don't let up. I devour her, wet and obscene, every flick and circle meant to make her lose control.

When I look up, she's watching me with wide, glassy eyes, lips parted, already ruined. I keep my mouth on her and growl against her flesh, "You taste like fucking sin, *ma colombe*. My sweet, dirty girl. I could live between these legs, drink you dry, and still want more."

Her head tips back, a strangled moan leaving her throat. I tighten my grip on her hips, pinning her down, tongue working her until she's trembling so hard the table groans beneath her. I swallow every sound, every shiver, until she finally breaks—coming on my tongue, shaking, whimpering my name like a confession.

Only then do I lift my head, my mouth shining with her, before I speak—my voice a dark promise.

"That was the first course," I growl, thumb dragging over her swollen lips. "Now, I'll fuck you on this table—and soon you'll be begging to choke on my cock until you forget your name."

She whimpers.

I stand, unbuckle my belt with a slow rasp of leather. With a rough yank, I flip her onto her stomach, pressing her down into the table. The chair falls and rattles from the force as I drag her hands behind her back and bind them tight with the belt, the leather biting into her skin.

"Stay still," I snarl, leaning over her ear. "I want you to remember exactly how it feels to be owned."

She complies like she's in a trance, chest pressed to the cool wood, breath fogging the table. I pull on the belt, cinching it tight enough that she gasps when the edges bite. The first mark will bloom there by the time I'm done—proof that she's mine.

I step closer to her, grip one of her hips hard enough to bruise while the other hand yanks on her bound wrists, forcing her shoulders to arch off the table, and slide my weeping cock inside her in one brutal, claiming thrust.

The sound she makes is half shock, half surrender. I drive into her again and again, the slap of skin and the low grind of my growl filling the room. The edge of the table bites into the soft flesh of her hips—marks that will bloom for days, my signature pressed into her skin.

Each thrust forces a small cry from her lips, until the only words she can form are "please" and my name.

When I lean over her, mouth at her ear, my voice is pure sin. "You'll see those bruises tomorrow and remember exactly who you belong to. Every mark, every ache, every fucking breath—mine."

Her body tightens around me, trembling as she falls apart a second time. I follow, dragging my teeth across her shoulder as I spill into her, pulse after pulse until we're both shaking.

For a long moment, all I can hear is our ragged breathing. I feel her wrists straining against the belt. Then I loosen it, watching the faint burn of leather bloom across her skin. I turn her face toward me, thumb brushing her lip, voice rough.

"Tell me, *ma colombe*—do you regret choosing me as your devil?"

She meets my gaze, eyes dark and dazed, and whispers, "No."

"*Ma colombe*, even if you ran to the ends of the fucking earth... I'd still be the one to tuck you in."

TIME SETTLES DIFFERENTLY HERE.

A week passes in the cadence I decide: late mornings tangled in sheets, afternoons at the table with packages arriving from half the continent, nights with the fire low and her in the lingerie I chose. *Ma poupée*, learning to wear silk like a second skin because I like the way it clings to her curves when she walks.

By the end of the first week, I've fucked her in every room and on every surface in the cabin. Her wrists have been bound more than they haven't. She knows what I want before I ask. She opens for me before I touch her. And every time I take her, I remind her who she belongs to—until there's not a single inch of her that hasn't been marked by me.

She bratted once—about the phone. A throwaway comment while scrolling, half-smirk on her lips, that she might call her father "*just to see what happens.*"

I didn't smile. I took the phone from her hand, set it aside, and told her to kneel.

She thought I was bluffing.

Two hours, I kept her there. Stripped down to nothing but my grip in her hair. Every time she whimpered that she'd be good, I pressed her closer, my thigh slick from the tears, snot, and spit she smeared against me. Then I brought her to the edge again and again, fingers fucking her until she was shaking so hard she could barely stay upright—then stopping just before she tipped over.

By the first hour, she was begging. By the second, she was sobbing my name into my skin like a prayer, her voice cracked and raw. When I finally let her come, it was with my mouth at her ear, telling her she'd asked for this, that I'd give her exactly what she begged for.

And when it was over, I didn't just leave her crumpled on the floor. I pulled her into my lap, her face buried against my chest, my hand stroking her damp hair until her breathing slowed. I pressed water to her lips, made her sip until her throat could work again, murmured soft French endearments into the crown of her head while her body trembled against me.

"You think I break you, *ma colombe*," I whispered against her hair, "but I'm the one who has to put you back together."

She clung like she didn't know if she was allowed—and I let her.

After that night, she stopped pretending she didn't crave the control.

The rules become ritual—but not cages. She doesn't dress without me choosing, not because I forbid her, but because she likes the way my eyes darken when I pick something for her. She doesn't come without permission, not because I'd punish her if she slipped, but because she likes asking, likes the way I make her wait until she's writhing and then praise her when she breaks. She doesn't close our bedroom door unless I'm inside, not because she's locked out of her own space, but because she's learned she sleeps easier when I'm there.

And every day, she gives me another sliver of herself. Sometimes with a glare, sometimes with a sigh, sometimes with a shy smile when she thinks I'm not looking. But always with that hunger in her eyes—like she's starting to understand she can lean on me as much as she fights me.

I watch her shoulders relax when I brush her hair after a shower. I hear the way her voice steadies when she practices French words with me, my hand warm over hers guiding the page. I feel the way she melts against me at night when I pull her close, like she's finally found a place to rest.

I press my lips to her hair, breathing her in. "*Chut.* Let me worship you the way you deserve."

She exhales, a quiet little sound that feels like surrender. Not the kind I wring out of her on her knees, but the kind that tells me she trusts me with more than her body. That she's letting me hold the weight she's carried alone for too long.

I don't tell her I like it just as much as when she glares at me, fights me, claws at me. That the softness is the part I never thought I'd want, never thought I'd need. But I keep her pressed against me anyway, my hand steady on her spine, until her breathing evens out and she slips into sleep.

***

WHAT I LIKE MOST isn't the way she breaks for me—it's the way she lives for me.

Her eyes aren't dead anymore. When I first saw her, she moved like a ghost in silk, smiling politely while her soul drowned behind her gaze. Now, every time she looks at me, there's light. Sharp, hungry, alive. And I'd kill anyone who tried to take it away.

She laughs more than I expected. Sometimes at me, sometimes at nothing at all—just a burst of sound in the kitchen while she pulls a tray of cookies out of the oven, or when she stirs sauce on the stove and sings off-key to a song she left playing. She hums without thinking, little melodies under her breath like she doesn't even realize her body is spilling joy into the room.

She turns the music up loud sometimes, bare feet on the wood floor, hips swaying while she dances with a spoon in her hand. *Ma poupée*, spinning in circles with flour dusting her cheek, laughing like no one's watching—even though I always am.

The cage I built for her—off-grid, hidden, mine—has become more freedom than the life her family caged her in. Here, no one is selling her, silencing her, or telling her who to be. Here, she wears silk because I like it, not because society demanded it. Here, she bakes because she wants to, hikes because she wants to, sings because she wants to.

She doesn't see it yet, not fully—but I've given her more than captivity. I've given her air. And every laugh, every hum, every sway of her body in my kitchen tells me I was right.

She was never alive until I caged her.

8

SOMETHING BLUE

SAVANNAH

THE TELEVISION IS A dull, blue-lit rectangle in the corner of the room, a presence rather than furniture—noise for company when the house hums too loudly. I have it on because silence is loud and because sometimes the world feels less threatening when I can put a glass wall between myself and it.

Today the glass wall cracks.

My mother is on the screen first—pale, hair pinned too tightly, voice frayed at the edges. "If anyone sees my daughter, please—please tell law enforcement where she is. We just want her home. We don't want this to end in tragedy."

Shame burns behind my ribs the way a match sets tinder. Their faces are all familiar: my aunt clutching a tissue, my cousin's mascara staining her cheek, the pastor wearing the same expression he used at funerals—the official, hollow sympathy of people who believe the correct answer to every crisis is to kneel and pray and call the police. My father doesn't speak; his jaw works like a machine trying to process an instruction he won't follow. They look like me, and in the same breath they don't.

They don't understand I left of my own will. They don't know how loud the cage had become.

I sit frozen as the anchor's voice folds into their pleas—"...and of course, if you know anything at all, contact the police..."—and then, as if someone has slid a needle into my chest and spun it, I can no longer breathe.

It happens fast. A hiss behind my breastbone, a pressure that folds my ribs inward. My fingers go numb. The light in the room pools wrong, and the carpet becomes a moving ocean. I stand because my knees stiffen, because sitting makes the world close in more—bad logic I can't argue with.

"Savannah?" Leon's voice at the doorway is a silhouette of sound—quiet, practiced, as if he has rehearsed this entrance ten times.

I try for a laugh. It chokes into something animal. "They're—" I point, uselessly, toward the blue glow.

He crosses the room with the calm of a man who knows precisely which walls will fall and where the cracks hide. He doesn't approach me like someone who has to ask permission; he approaches like someone who has authority to choose solidity. I want to recoil from that a little, and another stranger in me, a small practiced animal, leans into the certainty.

When he takes my hands it is firm but not rough. He pulls me toward him and I let myself be pulled because at this moment ease is a negotiation I do not trust myself to win.

"*Regarde-moi*," he says—*look at me*. "Breathe, *ma colombe*. Breathe."

I try to match his breath. In—two seconds. Out—three. The numbers are a scaffolding he offers to my collapsing lungs. Tears start behind my eyes and spill over, hot and relentless. I hate that they're on his shirt; I hate that they exist at all.

On the screen, my grandfather's voice cracks—he is begging, pleading not to the camera but to whoever was watching as if the show is the only altar he knows. My throat tightens again. I feel small and traitorous and enormous all at once.

I remember the last months at "home" like an unhealed bruise. The dinners where laughter had become monitoring, the phone calls felt like examinations, the way a glance from my father used to be a measurement of my worth. I remember the litany of "shoulds." *You should call; you should be grateful; you should forgive; you should act like a lady.* "Should" had a way of pressing down on me until my joints ached.

Leon keeps me upright. He doesn't let me fumble for words. "You're okay," he murmurs, though it's not a lie to soothe—it's a positioning. "You chose to leave. You are here because you chose to be."

Those words are small, precise stones; they roll inside my ribs and help build a little foundation.

My breathing slows. The world is not fixed, but it is negotiable. He leads me to the sofa and sits beside me, one arm around my shoulders like a brace. I curl into the space he makes as if my limbs have forgotten how to hold themselves up.

The TV continues—they say the same things, they hurt me the same way over and over. My mother says my name and it is used like a key, then a weapon. Then the anchor says something about "concerned family members" and suddenly there is a lawman's picture overlaid on the bottom corner of the screen, a phone number blinking.

"Turn it off," I whisper, barely audible.

Leon doesn't hesitate. The room goes quiet with the click. The silence that follows is heavy in a different way—less invasive, more attentive.

He holds me while the shaking comes and goes. He doesn't tell me to stop. He doesn't tell me I should be stronger. He lets me be messy and loud and human. When the hyperventilation eases he guides me through a grounding exercise—naming five things in the room, feeling the texture of the cushion, telling him the color of the curtains. He makes the practice businesslike and then softer, because he understands the difference.

He keeps holding me until the tremors fade into something slower, stranger. The same hands that steadied my breathing start tracing lazy circles on my wrists—right over the pulse points he marked last night.

Bruised and tender, the skin there still stings when he touches it. But the sting keeps me *here*. Keeps me real.

He murmurs, "Stay with me, *ma colombe*."

And I do. Because when the world feels like it's closing in, he doesn't tell me to calm down—he gives me something else to lose myself in.

The belt loops around my wrists, the smell of worn leather and skin sharp in the air, the scrape of it every time I pull against the restraint. He ties my hands to the small table next to the couch, pressing me into the cushions. His voice is low, steady. He tells me not to move, not to make a sound, not to come until he says.

He uses everything within reach to ground me—the soft drag of his tongue, the blunt press of his fingers, then he chooses to use the damn television remote.

I don't fully comprehend what he's doing until I feel it—smooth plastic pushing into me, the shape of it foreign and perfect. The ridges of the buttons scrape lightly against the sensitive inner walls, every raised edge catching on nerves until I gasp. Cool, unrelenting, it slides deeper as my body clenches around it. The tiny click of shifting buttons presses into me, sharp enough to make my breath hitch, grounding me in sensation instead of panic.

He watches me unravel, whispering filthy French praise against my throat, keeping me just shy of release until the tears turn from fear to want. Until the only thing left in my chest is him.

When he finally lets me come, it isn't permission—it's mercy.

He kisses up my body until his fingers tilt my chin up, his gaze dragging over my face like he's memorizing the aftershocks.

"You see?" he says quietly. "I don't take your pain away, *ma colombe*. I just teach it where to kneel."

And it works.

He is both the hand that locks the cage and the hand that frees me.

"You need to talk to someone, love," he says after a while. "Not me. Someone who is not *in* this—someone who understands. I will find someone."

I laugh again. It's brittle. How could anyone understand? I am a woman who left her family, with a man most of society despises, who seems to have traded safety for a life they can't measure.

"They will tell you what I say," I retort. "It'll make it all worse."

He lifts my chin with a finger, his thumb brushing the ridge of my jaw. "No, you will have your privacy, your agency. I will find someone who understands you are an adult and made your choice. Someone who will challenge you but not punish you for it. Do you want me to do that?"

I imagine therapists like grumpy gatekeepers—paper-stuffed and patronizing. I imagine yet another person telling me what I should have done, what I failed to do, or how to fix myself for the convenience of others.

But there is a gentleness in the way he says it. There is a fierce insistence that whatever I am is worth the investment. That in itself says something about him I hadn't let myself see—he wants me whole, not controlled.

He makes calls that night. He speaks into the phone with a tone I know like a blade—efficient, exact, with the soft impression of threat when he does not get what he wants immediately. He asks for a recommendation and then another, his questions are clinical.

Do they work with adults who have family estrangement?

Have they worked with clients who made autonomous decisions that others saw as risky?

Can they support someone in crisis and exhaust all other measures, before escalating to legal guardianship?

There is a rhythm to his interrogation that makes the edges of my anxiety dull. It becomes a battle plan and I like battle plans—solid, ordered, manageable.

He gives me options the next morning. Three names, three faces, three different kinds of competence. He tucks a folded page of notes into my palm like an offering. "You pick. You decide."

I study the small paragraphs about each woman. Dr. Henley—clinical, publications, a reputation for working with trauma and family estrangement. Mara Saint—community-focused, warm in photos, speaks multiple languages. Lise Varela—who lists "autonomy and adult decision-making" explicitly on her practice page. I run my finger down the lines and choose Lise because I like the word "autonomy."

At my first virtual appointment the screen flickers to life, her office visible in the background—bookshelves, plants that look like they've survived more than a season, a mug steaming on the desk. Lise Varela is younger than I expected. She has an easy gaze through the webcam, looking at me as if she sees the scaffolding behind my composure instead of mistaking it for completeness.

She does not coddle me. She does not glare at my choices like a disappointed parent. Instead, she listens with the precision of someone taking notes for a story she doesn't yet understand but intends to honor. When I tell her my family is on television looking for me, her face softens but does not shift to instructive concern.

"You left because you needed to," she says after I ramble through the months that led to my leaving. "People will always try to fit your reasons into their own narratives. That is not your responsibility to correct."

I want to correct her, to argue that perhaps I left for the wrong reasons. Maybe I was avoiding. Maybe I didn't know what I wanted. But there is a steadiness to Lise that invites nuance instead of accusation.

She asks questions I've never been asked. Never even contemplated.

What do you want when you're not trying to be someone else's version of safe?

What is your life when no one is watching?

How do you make a decision that isn't designed to placate others?

What is your vision of a perfect life?

Her curiosity is not indulgent—it is useful. I find myself answering honestly, because she doesn't appear shocked or scandalized. When I say I sometimes fear I chose badly, she nods, not surprised.

"Choice can be messy," she tells me. "It can be the best thing and the most dangerous thing at once. What we will do together is help you notice which decisions are aligning with who you want to be—not with who others think you should be."

I close my laptop with a file in my inbox—a plan. It is not a command. It's a map. Lise has given me homework that looks like small, mercifully practical tasks.

Write one paragraph about what you want in the next year.

Name three boundary statements you will practice

Call one person from your past life who you think might support you and tell them what you need.

It sounds like a modest rebellion.

Leon is waiting on the couch when I leave the bedroom. He looks at me like someone who has checked the simplest of boxes and found something better than he expected.

"How was she?" he asks. The question is deeper than curiosity—it's inventory. I realize, with an odd, sudden flash, that he is asking to measure the landscape to plan his part in it.

"She listened," I say. "She didn't try to fix me. She asked what I want. She gave me homework."

He nods, like a man hearing a favorable report from a scout. "Good. We'll do the work. Together."

There is a tenderness in his voice that is not ownership so much as promise. But the promise has teeth—he will protect me, yes, but not incarcerate me. He will keep me safe from those who would make decisions for me, but also from the impulses that would undo me.

At night, lying against him, I replay scenes in my head. I can still feel Lise's gaze—steady, piercing, honest. I can also feel the heat of my family's faces frozen on the television screen, and a tiny, unpleasant kernel of shame that will take longer to unspool. But I need space to be messy. I need someone who will meet me there without making me small for it.

I fall asleep with my head on his chest and the television dark. Outside, the forest hums with quiet possibility.

His hand slides over my hair and he murmurs, "I protect what is mine, *ma colombe*. I'll even protect you from yourself."

The words are dangerous and oddly comforting. I am learning the shape of his protection. This is not a locked cage but a border, held by fierce hands that will keep the wolves away but not the wind. I breathe, and for the first time in weeks, the breath feels like mine.

***

THE NEXT MORNING, SUNLIGHT cuts across the bed in soft gold. I stir first, but Leon shifts beside me, eyes half-open, watching. For once he doesn't reach for control, doesn't issue a command. He touches me like I'm breakable, a slow slide of his hand down my hip, his mouth pressing reverent kisses along my shoulder.

It's un-Leonlike, this patience, this gentleness that borders on worship. He moves over me with unhurried intent, giving me every chance to turn away, every chance to breathe into the space between us. My body arches, my fingers clutch, not from fear but from want. He sinks into me slowly, filling, stretching, holding me steady as if he can anchor every fracture.

Our rhythm is quiet, tender, yet open—my moans caught against his throat, his breath warm against my ear. No sharp edges. Only him, only me, only this.

When I shatter around him it's not with panic but release. The sob that escapes is different—less grief, more relief. He whispers against my hair, "*Ma colombe*... you're safe. You're mine." And the words feel like freedom.

After, he keeps me pressed to his chest, both of us damp with sweat and sunlight. I realize then—with a clarity sharper than any fear—that choosing him wasn't madness. It was survival. It was mine.

9

FOR BETTER OR WORSE

LEON

One night, she falls asleep early on the couch in a pale slip I'd laid out for her.

Bare legs, bare shoulders, the fire painting her in gold. She's not just tired—she's come down from the ragged edge of a panic attack.

It hit fast. One minute, she was curled beside me with her head on my shoulder, the next she was shaking, breath stuttering like her ribs were closing in on her. I'd cupped her face, made her look at me.

"*Regarde-moi.*" Kept my voice low and steady until her eyes focused. I counted for her while she took deep breaths.

Then I got her two Xanax from the stash in the bathroom, a glass of cold water from the fridge. Held the glass while she drank because her hands wouldn't stop trembling.

When it was over, she'd leaned into me like she didn't want to let go. I didn't let her.

Now she's more than "just" asleep—she's adrift, soft and loose-limbed, her breathing deep and slow. I lift her into my arms and carry her to bed, careful not to wake her. My palm drifts over her thigh, up the curve of her hip—slow, claiming, inevitable.

I've told her before that she's mine whenever I want her, and she agreed—explicitly. No games. No hesitation.

Ma colombe, I'd never touch you without your consent—lucky for me, you already gave it to me when you gave me yourself.

I ease the slip higher, my knuckles brushing the heat between her thighs. She shifts in her sleep, a soft sound catching in her throat. *So fucking warm.* My palm cups her cunt through the damp silk of her panties, the fabric clinging to her like it's desperate to keep me out.

Pathetic. I hook my fingers in the lace and drag it down her legs, slow enough to enjoy the view. Now she's bare—my pretty little cunt open to me.

Ma parfaite petite pute. I drag a single finger down her slit, slow enough to feel the wet glisten coat my skin. She's soaked. Not dreaming of anything else—just me. Always me.

I part the folds of her cunt and circle her clit, gentle, taunting, until her hips tilt toward me without her even waking. Her body knows me now, reacts like it's been trained to respond to nothing but my touch.

Even in sleep, her pulse stutters under my lips, her thighs shifting open, needy.

Then I push a finger inside her, slow, savoring the tight clutch of her heat. Another joins it, and I start to fuck her with them in a steady rhythm that makes her whimper in her sleep. Her cunt clings greedily, wet and perfect, already weeping for me. So fucking good, *ma colombe*. I curl my fingers, finding that spot inside that makes her seize around me like she's begging me not to stop, even if she doesn't have words for it.

Her slip slides off one shoulder, baring the curve of her breast, pale against the firelight. I bend down and take her nipple into my mouth, sucking until it stiffens under my tongue. She arches into me instinctively, a half-asleep gasp escaping her parted lips. I keep fucking her with my fingers, deeper, harder, curling with every thrust until her cunt grips like a fist around me, as though her body knows I'll never stop until she's wrung dry.

She's my own Sleeping Beauty—laid out for me, helpless and holy, caught between dreams and my hands. Every twitch, every breath, every broken sound from her throat is mine to orchestrate. I never want her to wake to anything less than my mouth, my fingers, or my cock claiming her.

Then she moans my name and my fire turns into an inferno.

"*Je parie que tu rêves de moi*," I growl against her skin. "You dream of me. You wanted this."

Her hips roll, chasing me, and I speed up, fucking her harder with my hand, my thumb grinding over her clit until her whole body tightens. Her orgasm rips through her with a muffled cry, her cunt milking my fingers like it's begging me not to stop.

I don't give her more. Not yet.

I pull my fingers out, slick with her release, and slide them past my lips, tasting almost every drop. *Tu m'as dans la peau, ma colombe.* Then I press them to her lips. Her tongue works in her sleep, sucking me clean like a good little slut.

"That's my good girl," I murmur. "Every time you come, it's a vow."

My fingers sink back into her heat, slow and deep, while my other hand wraps around my cock. I work myself almost to the edge before I replace my fingers with my cock, sliding into the hilt like it's where I've always belonged. I spill into her, grinding it deeper, marking her from the inside out. This cunt is the only altar worthy of my release—whether she's awake to feel it or not.

That night is just one of many liberties I take with her.

***

DAYS TAKE ON THE rhythm I set. Mornings start with her on her knees between my legs, not for me to fuck her mouth—but for me to feed her breakfast and stroke her hair, kissing her lips between bites. Afternoons, I keep her otherwise bare under one of my shirts or a silk slip while she pads through the cabin doing the small tasks I give her.

She folds my clothes, polishes my boots, sits on the couch with her knees spread while we both read—which usually results in my fingers finding her before I finish a chapter.

I learn to live for the small moments.

Her lips glossy with honey from the spoon I press between them.

The sound of my belt sliding free before I bind her wrists to the headboard.

Her muffled cry when I pull her hair to make her look at me while she comes.

She brats now and then, enough to keep it interesting. Once, she rolled her eyes when I told her to kneel.

I didn't let it slide. I made her stand against the wall, hands locked behind her back, chest rising and falling like she knew what was coming for her. I strapped a vibrator to her. It was tight between her thighs, humming low against her cunt, and I stood behind her, mouth close to her ear, feeding her orders she pretended she didn't need.

"You won't come until you beg," I told her. My hand slid down her belly, palm flat over the toy, pressing it harder against her clit. She shuddered, biting her lip, refusing to give me the satisfaction of a sound.

Ten minutes in, she was trembling. Thirty minutes in, she was panting, her thighs slick and trembling, sweat running down her spine. An hour, and she broke—sobbing *s'il te plaît* like it was a confession, her head tipped back against my shoulder, tears streaking her cheeks.

The French undid me. I unbuckled the straps, slowly peeling the toy away from her soaked cunt, my fingers immediately sliding into her. "So fucking wet for me," I growled, curling deep until she gasped. I fucked her with my fingers while I spun her to face me, my other hand gripping her throat, making her keep her eyes on mine. "*Regarde-moi.*"

She clung to my shirt as I shoved my cock into her, lifting her against the wall, her legs wrapping around my waist. Every thrust drove a cry from her throat, every slap of my hips against hers echoing in our quiet home. I bent my head, biting her neck hard enough to leave a bruise, fucking her harder until she was crying out my name, begging for release.

"Beg louder," I snarled, grinding my cock deep, my thumb ruthless on her clit. "Let me hear how bad you need it."

"Please, Leon—please—" her voice cracked, desperate, broken. That was all it took. Her cunt clamped down around me like a vice, her whole body arching in surrender as I fucked her through the orgasm, spilling into her with a groan torn straight from my chest.

When it was over, I didn't drop her. I carried her to the bed, laid her down, and pulled a blanket over her shaking body. Her cheeks were still wet with tears, eyes glassy, lips swollen. I kissed her hair, held a glass of water to her mouth, stroked her thigh until the tremors faded.

"*Ma colombe,*" I murmured, brushing her damp hair back, "I will always put you back together."

She nestled against me, soft and pliant, her breathing evening out. And I let her, because she'd earned it.

✳✳✳

THEN THERE ARE MORE moments—more memories.

Her thighs trembling while I hold her just at the edge, smirking at her pleas.

Her scent clinging to my fingers when I let her taste herself.

The slick heat of her cunt when I slide my cock in after hours of denial.

Some nights, I let her think she's in control—straddling my lap, grinding against me like she can get herself off without my permission. She never makes it. I grip her hips, still her movement, make her say she belongs to me before I give her what she's chasing.

Other nights, I take her knees to the floor and teach her how to use her mouth the way I like. I sit back in the chair, legs spread, my cock heavy in my fist as I beckon her forward.

"Eyes up. *Regarde-moi.*"

I guide her pace with my grip in her hair, making her breathe through her nose, making her take me deeper, until her throat works around me and her eyes shine with tears. I tell her when to lick, when to suck, when to hold me in her mouth and just breathe. By the time I'm done, she knows the difference between *trying* to please me and *actually* pleasing me.

Her eyes continue to change. I notice it more each day—less dead, more alive, less defiance, more hunger. She still pretends she hates some of it, still tosses me sharp little glares, but her body betrays her every time.

When I tell her to spread, she spreads. When I tell her to look at me, she does. And when I tell her to come for me, she obeys like it's the only command she's ever wanted to hear.

I fall in love with her more and more.

Her whisper of "yes, Sir" against my throat.

The way her back arches when my teeth sink into her shoulder.

The broken sound she makes when I whisper, "Every time you come, it's a vow."

Weeks blur into each other. By the fourth, she is kneeling without being told, her French sharper, her bratting rarer.

She's not just following the rules. She's anticipating them. Pouring my coffee before I ask. Sleeping in the lingerie I lay out for her, even when I don't touch her.

But not everything she does revolves around me or sex. Sometimes she curls up in the corner of the couch in leggings and a hoodie, legs tucked beneath her, lost in whatever show she's binging while I work at the table. She looks so fucking young like that—hair in a messy knot, eyes wide at the screen—I catch myself staring instead of reading reports.

We watch movies together, too. My arm slung over the back of the sofa, her legs stretched across my lap. Half the time I don't even care what's on the screen—I care about the way she absently strokes my thigh when she's caught up in the story, or the way she buries her face against me when the tension gets too high.

I make her practice her French. She pretends to hate it, glaring at the flashcards, groaning when I correct her. But when she finally nails a phrase, when she says it smooth and right, she laughs—bright and surprised, like she forgot she was allowed to be proud of herself. That sound does more to me than her moans ever could.

We hike the ridges around the property, boots crunching on gravel and pine needles, her hand in mine as we point out wildflowers sprouting between the rocks. Sometimes deer flash through the trees, white tails vanishing into green shadows, and she gasps like it's magic. I tell her the names of plants in French, make her repeat them until she rolls her eyes and then smiles anyway.

She has started baking—something she never did before, though she told me once she always wanted to. Now the kitchen smells like bread or cookies, warm and rich, drifting down the hall before I even set foot inside. She'll stand there with flour all over, humming to herself, and look up at me like she's waiting for approval. I don't give it with words. I give it by pinning her against the counter and tasting sugar off her lips.

And through all of it, she never wants for anything. Not food. Not warmth. Not freedom—not the kind they gave her, anyway. The cage I've built keeps her, but it also lets her breathe.

She never wants for anything—she never will.

And every time I fuck her—whether with my fingers, my mouth, or my cock—I leave the same truth with her:

Every time you come, it's a vow.

10

THE RUNAWAY BRIDE

SAVANNAH

I USED TO THINK I'd count the minutes until he left the room. Now, I count the ones until he comes back.

It snuck up on me—this insatiable hunger. At first it was just survival, a truce I told myself I had to keep until I found a way for my brain to override my heart and body. I thought he was just a rebellion, something reckless to prove to myself I could make my own choices—that eventually I'd crave the familiarity of home, of servants, of freedom to go anywhere on my own. That eventually I'd work him out of my system.

But the more I learn the edges of him, the more I like the way they cut.

Six weeks in, I realize it's worse than hunger. It's dependence. I breathe easier when I hear his boots on the porch. My body reacts to his shadow crossing a doorway like it's a promise.

Leon can be all sharp steel and cold eyes, but when he wraps a blanket around my shoulders or brushes my hair back from my face, it feels like a vow.

"*Chut. Laisse moi prendre soin de toi comme tu le mérites.*"

The words roll through me in a low, accented murmur that turns my bones to heat.

I tell myself I shouldn't want that. That I shouldn't melt for the man who took me, caged me, made my world so small it's just him. But when he's gone—even for an hour—I feel the walls press in without him to fill the space.

That's why, one day when my brain starts to win, when the opportunity comes, I run. I run barefoot, the ground brutal beneath me, every root and stone cutting into tender skin until it feels like fire searing up my legs. My lungs burn, each gasp a knife in my chest, my muscles screaming with the strain of going farther, faster, anywhere but back to him. Branches claw at my arms and whip across my face, leaving welts, my hair snarled with pine needles as I push deeper into the forest with no sense of direction. I'm lost, but I don't dare slow down. My breath tears ragged from my chest, feet slick with dirt and blood, vision swimming with panic.

Just when I think I've bought myself distance, I hear the heavy slam of a door, the purposeful, steady strike of boots pounding after me—measured, merciless, inevitable. He's coming, and the sound of him gaining ground is more terrifying than any nightmare. My stride falters, my chest heaving, and before I can twist away his hand clamps around my wrist, molten air crackling between us.

He doesn't drag me back inside. He slams me into the rough bark of an oak so hard the breath rushes out of me, pinning my arms above my head until my shoulders strain.

His breath is a low, feral snarl against my ear, hot enough to burn. "Ma *parfaite petite pute*... you think you can run from me?"

The words are more promise than question—low and lethal, curling through me like smoke. He rips my shirt in one brutal pull, the violent snap of fabric echoing in the stillness until it sounds like the only thing in the world. The shreds twist tight around my wrists, the makeshift rope biting deep enough to send hot sparks racing up my arms, each one a reminder that I'm caught—claimed. Quickly, those wrists are bound to the tree trunk above my head.

The forest swallows my gasp, but he hears it, and his mouth drags along my neck in a slow graze that's more threat than kiss.

His thigh drives between mine with punishing force, pinning me in place, pressing until I'm shaking with the effort not to grind down on him, every nerve ending screaming for friction.

"You want freedom, *ma colombe*?" he breathes, voice dark silk over steel. "I'll give you the kind of freedom you'll crawl back to me for, bleeding and begging."

My inner voice should be screaming, clawing for control, but it's drowned out by the deep, aching throb between my legs and the dizzy rush of knowing he'll take what he wants, exactly how he wants, and I'll savor every goddamn second of it.

By the time his fingers slide under my shorts, I'm feral with desire. The bark bites into my spine like it's engraving his claim there; my pulse pounds so loud it drowns out the wind. Every stroke is an act of ownership, a brand burned into my flesh; every pause, a cruel, deliberate punishment that makes me whimper and strain against my binds for more.

He strips me bare in the night air, peeling away each layer like it's his right, his fingers brushing over my skin in a slow, possessive sweep as if he's memorizing every freckle, every scar, every curve that belongs to him now. The gentle wind prickles over me, but his gaze is hotter than the sun, devouring me without hurry, making me shiver in ways that have nothing to do with the cold.

Then he drops to his knees like a worshipper before an altar, his hands anchoring my hips as his mouth claims me—slow at first, drawing out teasing licks that make my toes curl into the damp earth, his breath warm against my slickness. Then he grows ruthless, sucking and tasting like he's starving for me, his tongue stroking in a rhythm that has me panting, until my hips are rolling against him shamelessly, seeking more pressure, more of him.

I'm teetering on the edge, my vision spotted, my knees weak—when the sudden cold kiss of metal replaces his mouth. I gasp, a sound swallowed by the forest, as I realize he has drawn the gun from the holster at his spine. The barrel trails deliberately up my inner thigh, leaving a chilled path over my heated skin, before pressing against my slick core in obscene contrast.

The steel is unyielding and indecent, as he pushes just enough to breach me—slow, deliberate, feeding it into me inch by inch until I can feel my heartbeat thudding against it. He begins to fuck me with the gun in controlled thrusts, each one a statement of absolute power, as though he owns not just my body but the very air I breathe.

My head falls back against the bark, my bound wrists tugging at the restraint, every shallow pump a reminder of exactly how dangerous he is—how easily this weapon could end me—and how little I want to escape.

My heart slams against my ribs. It's the only sound I hear until the click of the safety. That sound should freeze me, should leave me petrified. But it doesn't. The threat, the fear, only heightens my arousal.

My mind is screaming somewhere far away, but my toes curl, traitorous, as the cold steel presses into me. My fingers flex, bracing for pain, craving something I can't even begin to name.

He adjusts the angle, pressing deeper until the cold steel is warmed and the bite of it is replaced by a burn of friction that blurs the edges of my vision. My breath catches on a ragged sob that melts into a low, desperate moan, my body clutching greedily around the metal as if it's the only thing tethering me to earth.

Every muscle is taut, every nerve strung between terror and ecstasy, and it should split me open with fear. Instead, the danger continues to flood me with molten heat, my mind screaming somewhere far away while my soul arches into the peril, pleading for more, for harder, for him—*always him.*

He smirks against my skin, reminding me of his power without a single word, the curve of his mouth wicked as if he's reading every filthy thought racing through my head. Then he drops the weapon with a deliberate thud into the leaves, hands finding my hips in a bruising grip before he hoists me effortlessly, my bound wrists still very much secure.

My back scrapes against the bark with every shift, the sting only sharpening the pleasure as he spears into me in one hard thrust. The force knocks a gasp from my lungs, my legs clamping around his waist as if I could hold him inside me forever. He fucks me rough and relentless—each movement an unspoken decree that I am his, until my moans turn to ragged cries.

The world dissolves into heat, bark, and the sound of his low, guttural groans as he chases his own release. When he finally spends himself, spilling deep, he stays there for a long moment, his breath hot against my throat, before unbinding me, the tattered shirt falling away from my wrists. His arms slide under me as if I'm the lightest thing he's ever held and he carries me inside like I'm fragile porcelain—but we both know I'm already broken and rebuilt in his hands.

He sets me down on the edge of the kitchen counter, the cool marble shocking against my overheated skin, the contrast making me shiver as he braces me there, steadying me as if I might float—or fall—away from him.

His hands are sure, unhurried, holding me in place while his gaze sweeps over every mark, every scrape, with the kind of focus that feels more intimate than the sex we just had.

The sting of disinfectant follows the warmth of his lips ghosting over each scrape on my back, the alcohol bite tempered by the softness of his mouth. His touch lingers, fingers tracing the curve of my spine before he bends closer, his breath fanning across my ear as he speaks.

His voice is low, velvet and steel, a litany of soft French endearments, possessive oaths, and dark promises that I'm safe because I'm his—that no one will ever touch me without bleeding for it, that I will never spend another night wondering who would come for me if I screamed.

The truth is, I love the pain. I spent so much of my life numb—unable to feel anything—the pain feels real. It lets me know that Leon is real, that his touch is real, that I'm alive.

I don't mean to say it, but the words slip out, fractured and raw, torn from somewhere deeper than thought: "Don't let me go." My voice shakes, but the truth in it doesn't. The admission terrifies me almost as much as it relieves me. Because for all the blood and fire, for all the ways he's broken me down, I don't want freedom. I want him.

His answer is silence at first, heavy and certain. He holds me against him, lips brushing my shoulder but no words, only the weight of his presence, as though he's letting me sit in the truth of the request.

My thoughts spiral.

I don't want him to release me.

Even if I could run again I'd pray for him to catch me.

The only thing more unbearable than being his is the thought of not being his at all.

At last, his voice rumbles low against my skin. "One day, *ma colombe*, I'll make you my wife. Not in a church full of your father's friends. Not with papers and promises that mean nothing. I'll chain you to me, vows made in blood, and no god will be able to take you away."

The words should scorch me. Instead they sink into bone, into breath, into want. I turn my face toward him, my whisper shaking but sure. "I want that. I want you. However you take me for yourself."

The faint curl of his lips against my skin seals it. He doesn't let me go, not then, not ever—and the vow in his stillness is louder, darker, more binding than any priest's blessing could be

****

WEEKS BLEED INTO MONTHS, each one reshaping me in ways I didn't know I wanted.

He lets me fill my hours with what I choose—first baking, the kitchen filled with the scent of cinnamon and sugar, my fingers dusted in flour as he leans in the doorway, watching like I'm the most fascinating thing he's ever seen. Then painting, where I lose myself for hours in the sweep of a brush, splattering colors onto canvas until my skin carries flecks of red, gold, and blue. Sometimes he stands behind me, his arms crossed against his chest, murmuring in French about how I look when I create—how I was made for beauty and for him.

It takes longer than he seems to have wanted, but one afternoon, a package arrives—long, heavy, and unmarked. Inside, nestled in silk, is the most beautiful cello I've ever touched.

Custom-made in Italy, the wood gleams like it holds sunlight captive, its curves sensual under my fingertips. My throat tightens, my chest aching as I realize what it means—that he's seen me, *really seen me*, in a way no one ever has.

He just says, "Play for me," and the command feels like a gift.

I do. That day. The next. Every day after.

Sometimes he makes me play for him clothed, poised like the dutiful student. But other times, he strips me bare, settles himself in a wide chair, and pulls me down between his spread legs. The cello rests against my chest, the cool wood pressing into hot skin, his thighs caging me as completely as his hands ever have.

His breath ghosts over my ear as he murmurs, "Don't lose your rhythm, *ma colombe*. If you falter, I'll make you start again." His fingers wander over my body while I play, slow strokes that test my concentration, pushing me to keep the bow steady even as my thighs tremble and my breath hitches. Every note becomes a moan disguised as music, every chord a vow. By the time the final note fades, I'm undone in his lap, strings still humming as he reminds me I belong to him.

When I'm not on his lap, the bow feels like an extension of my body, and the sound pours out rich and aching, echoing off the high beams of the house and into the quiet woods. He listens, always—sometimes with his eyes closed, sometimes with his gaze locked on me, as though the music binds me to him as much as his hands do.

I paint every day too, my canvases stacking against the walls, colors bleeding into one another like my old life bleeding away.

I breathe the clean mountain air, taste it in my lungs, hear nothing but the wind in the trees, the rustle of leaves, the low hum of his voice when he finds me and drags his knuckles along my jaw.

There is no pressure here but the heat of his hands. No demands except the ones he makes—and I welcome them. I've traded fake smiles and cocktail parties with men who played at power, for nights tangled in silk sheets with a man who *is* power.

And I am happier—dangerously, addictively happier—than I have *ever* been.

II

TILL DEATH

LEON

THE BOW GLIDES OVER the strings, slow and aching, drawing out a note that hangs in the air like a breath she's holding for me. She plays as if she's confessing, every movement of her wrist and every curve of her back telling me something she'll never say out loud. I lean against the doorway, unseen, letting the sound seep into me. It's a rare thing—something in this world that's still pure, untouched by blood or ruin. But purity doesn't last. Not around me.

They came for her, and she doesn't even know it. Not exactly her family—not yet. But men they hired. Three of them. Thought they could slip past the edge of my land, through my walls, without me knowing. They thought they could take what's mine. They should've done their fucking homework.

I step into her view and she watches me pull on my gloves and arm myself.

"Keep playing, *ma colombe*," I order quietly.

She nods as a shadow crosses the window and the note thins. The bow stumbles; the sound becomes a question. She doesn't stop playing—she keeps the melody alive with a trembling hand—but her head turns, slowly, and in that tiny tilt I see her recognize that something is very wrong.

They slip in like thieves, low on courage and high on the arrogance of men who believe the only thing that will meet them is the sound of the cello.

The first one barely has time to register my shadow before the blade slides between his ribs. I feel the vibration of steel meeting bone, the wet resistance as I push deeper. The copper sting of fresh blood hits my nose as cartilage pops, lungs collapsing under my slow twist. His breath comes out in a wet gargle, spraying warmth across my hand. I shove him off the steel, watching his eyes fix on nothing as he folds to the floor like discarded meat.

She goes pale and stops playing. Her hands shake, but she doesn't bolt. She watches as she stands.

When the second lunges, pulling a gun, the world sharpens to a single, brutal focus. I move like a machine that's been practiced on violence. I grab him and fold his elbow to his wrist—a hard, clean snap—the gun clattering across the floor. Pressing him to the nearest post, I let the old iron do the talking; two shots into the chest, one into the skull, the spray marking the aged wood like sacrament. She stumbles back a step, palms pressed to her mouth, but her eyes are fixed on me as if trying to memorize every angle.

The third I spend more time on. I drag him by the collar out to the truck they abandoned in the trees. The stink of sweat and panic filling my lungs, his knees grinding raw on the gravel. His blood—thick, metallic—already coats my gloves from the gash I opened with the butt of my gun. I force his palm open, carve my initials into the flesh with deliberate, sawing strokes, each letter a promise. His screams rip through the cold night air, bouncing off the dark tree line. When he jerks back, I drive my boot into his shin until I feel the give of bone beneath.

His breaths turn to wet, ragged sobs; blood slicks his arms, drips from his fingertips, pooling at his knees. He trembles, eyes wide, staring at me like I'm something other than human—something worse.

She meets my eyes—barefoot in the forest—with a look that is not fear at all but something closer to awe.

I crouch, smell his fear up close, tilting his chin with the barrel of my gun. "*Va leur dire ce que je fais aux hommes qui regardent ma femme.*" He swallows, throat working hard, the scent of blood and gun oil heavy between us.

I fire the gun into the ground right next to his head, then press the hot barrel to his cheek until his skin hisses.

"Go. Crawl back to the ones who sent you. Tell them exactly what waited for you here. *Elle m'appartient maintenant.* She belongs to me now."

He stumbles into the night, leaving a trail of blood like a wedding aisle. I watch him go until he's nothing but a shadow against the tree line.

When I look back at her, something new blooms across her face—raw, hungry, immediate. She audibly swallows, a small, private sound, and in that instant I know the truth.

The violence doesn't break her from me; it binds her more tightly.

By dawn, the abandoned church waits for us—cold stone and broken stained glass, a ruin dressed in shadows and silence. Every step inside feels like a trespass into something holy that forgot it was holy a long time ago. The morning light filters through fractured panes, casting splinters of red and gold across her skin.

I dress her in black lace, each fastening deliberate, a slow claiming dressed as a ritual. My fingers work over buttons and hooks as if sealing a vow with every touch. Her breathing shifts—shallow, expectant—but she stays quiet. Her wrists are bound in front of her, chains clinking softly with each step as I lead her down the aisle.

The sound echoes, a metallic chime in a place where prayers used to live. The air smells of dust, candle smoke, and something older—something like sacrilege, something that makes the blood in my veins thrum with possession.

I feel the satisfaction coil in my chest like a predator settling over its kill. This is not romance; it's reclamation. I've bled for her, killed for her, and now I'll brand her in a way the world can never scrub away.

At the altar, I take her picture before I wrap the chain tighter, the iron biting into her wrists until it leaves faint marks that will outlast the moment. She's framed by stone and shadow, looking like sin incarnate—my bride of blood.

I take in the sight, the contrast of the dark lace against pale skin, the defiance in her eyes warping into something darker. I capture another picture, knowing I will want it later.

"Repeat after me, *ma colombe*," I growl, but she shakes her head.

"I don't need you to tell me the words," she breathes, voice steady but thick with something raw, something real. Her eyes lock on mine as if she's piercing straight through the bone. "I vow to never belong to anyone else—not in body, not in breath, not in blood. I vow to wear your name like armor, to carry the weight of it without flinching, and let your darkness be my home, even when it burns." She tilts her chin, defiance and devotion tangled in the same heartbeat. "I vow to meet your fire with my own."

My chest tightens, feral heat tearing through me like shrapnel. I step closer until her chains rattle, until I can taste her breath. "And I vow to kill the world before I ever let it take you. I vow to love you the way fire loves oxygen—completely, until nothing is left. I vow to make your enemies choke on your name and to spill oceans of blood if it means you're mine and you keep breathing. You said forever, and I heard obedience.

You gave me your vows, and I'll bind you to me in flesh and steel."

Her lips curve, wicked and sure, but her voice softens just enough to slip the blade deeper. "Then I obey. Not because you tell me to, but because I've chosen the cage—and the man who owns the key."

I take her bound hands in mine, the iron clink of the chains echoing in the hollow church, and draw my knife. The metal catches the fractured light before I press the tip to the delicate skin of her wrist. The cut is shallow but deliberate, part kiss, part claim. Blood wells instantly—rich, red, alive—sliding over my fingers. The copper scent floods my head as I lift her wrist to my mouth. I drink slowly, letting the heat coat my tongue, the metallic tang sparking through me like electricity. Her pulse flutters hard against my lips, and she never looks away, her eyes locked on mine with unflinching devotion and defiance that makes me want to consume her whole.

Then I turn the blade on myself, dragging it across my own wrist. The sting is sharp, the heat immediate, a rush of my own lifeblood running free. I press our wounds together, skin to skin, the warmth mingling, our blood mixing until I can feel her inside me, and me inside her.

The bond thrums through my veins, ancient and savage. "We are bound now," I murmur, voice low and rough. "By blood, by will, by the ruin we choose. Nothing on this earth can unmake it."

I lift my wrist to her mouth, and she doesn't hesitate—not even for a heartbeat. Her lips part, hot breath on my skin, and then she's drinking. My blood coats her tongue, stains her lips dark, and drips slowly down her chin. I've never seen anything more beautiful—my mark inside her, my life painting her mouth. It streaks her throat like war paint.

My breath catches, harsh and hungry. "*Ma colombe,* you've never looked more mine than you do right now."

I step behind her, yanking the chains until her arms stretch so far forward they drag her down, her stomach and chest pressed flat against the cold altar. The bite of metal into her wrists forces a gasp from her throat, the sound raw and sharp in the hollow church.

My knife kisses the top of her shoulder, then trails down, slow and merciless, slicing through black lace. Threads part with a whisper, the dress falling away until pale skin gleams in the fractured light, bent and offered over the altar. I fist her hair, pulling her head back and facing her toward the cracked, looming cross above us.

"Look at it," I murmur against her ear, voice all gravel and sin. "Remember every false deity they ever tried to give you. Because from this moment on, I'm the only one you worship. Every prayer you have left belongs to me. Every time you come, it's a vow—and you will be making lots of vows over this altar."

Her gasp turns into a moan as I slide the knife lower, tracing the curve of her spine, pressing just enough for her to feel the cold kiss of the blade. I linger there, letting the sharp edge whisper over her skin before shifting my grip. She tenses but doesn't move away, trusting me in that dangerous way that makes my blood hum.

I draw the blade in a slow, deliberate path, making three shallow cuts along the slope of her back. Blood wells up in thin crimson lines, stark against her pale skin. I bow my head and lap at each one, my tongue following the trail before sealing my mouth over them to suck, pulling the copper-salt heat into me. She shivers under the attention, the chain at her wrists rattling with every breath.

I lift my head, my lips smeared with her blood, and murmur against her ear, "Still not enough of you, wife. I'll never have enough." My hands roam her sides possessively, feeling her tremble from the mingling sting and pleasure, and only then do I set the blade aside, the echo of danger still clinging to the air between us as I free my hands for what comes next.

My palms smooth down the curve of her ass, spreading her open to the fractured light, and I watch the way her body trembles. I slip one hand down her front and between her thighs, fingers finding her clit in slow, taunting circles, while my other hand works two fingers into her dripping cunt from behind. The wet heat grips me instantly, but I'm not done—my thumb presses against the tight ring of her untouched ass before I spit, the slickness sliding down to coat her. She tenses, so I push slowly, working my thumb inside her ass.

She jolts, gasping again, a raw sound that makes my cock ache. I lean down, lips brushing her ear. "My bride... my wife... you'll take me here soon. Both holes stretched for me, filled with me, worshiping me."

Blood from the earlier cuts, still slick on my skin and hers, mixes with the wetness between her thighs. The mess of spit, blood, and her arousal makes me harder.

I finger her deeper, curling inside her cunt while stretching her ass, letting the rhythm match the filthy words dripping from my mouth.

"I'll make you come like this, and then I'll fuck your ass until you can't remember any god but me."

My pace builds until her knees start to shake, until her chains clink with every thrust of my fingers. Her body quivers, her breath catches, and I feel her break apart around me, her climax spilling hot over my hand as my promises sink deep into her bones.

When I pull my fingers away, she lets out a desperate, broken whimper at the loss, hips rocking back in search of me.

I press my mouth to her temple, my voice a dark promise, as I whisper, "I'm not done with you, *ma femme*. Not even close."

I move slowly around the altar, boots echoing on the stone, until I'm in front of her. Her head tilts up when I grip her hair, forcing her to hold my gaze. I let her feel the weight of me, the heat against her mouth, before sliding my cock between her parted lips. The first glide is slow, testing the softness of her mouth, the way her tongue instinctively curls around me.

I murmur praise and filth in equal measure, letting each line drip into her like another claim. "Look at you, my bride—my perfect wife—laid out on your belly over a holy altar like an offering. Good girl... opening up so well for me."

My voice dips lower, filthier. "You're getting so good at this. Look at you, opening your throat for me like you were made to do it. Taking me like it's another vow you can't wait to keep."

Each thrust is deep, deliberate, my fingers tangled in her hair so I can guide her exactly where I want her. Her eyes never close, even when I push further, feeling her throat flex around me. I hold there, savoring the tight pull, before easing back just enough to let her drag in a breath through her nose. I release some cum, just a little, holding back most of it and it slicks her lips and tongue. I pull out and use my thumb to smear it wider, mixing with the blood on her lips and marking her.

My cock finds the very back of her throat again, and I keep her there longer than necessary, rocking my hips slowly at first, then harder, until her cheeks flush and her eyes glaze with the heady mix of oxygen deprivation and arousal. I groan when her throat relaxes completely for me, the sensation clawing up my spine. At the brink, I pull back sharply, letting the wet sound echo in the quiet church. I smear her spit and my cum across her lips and chin with the head of my cock, watching it glisten there like an unholy anointing, before stepping away, leaving her panting, wrecked, and waiting for more.

Back behind her, my fingers slide into her again—cunt and ass—until she's gasping for air, another climax tearing through her. Her wrists strain against the chains, her cheek pressed to the cold altar. I make her come three more times and only stop because she's panting like she's drowning on dry land.

I pull my thumb from her ass and curl three of my fingers deeper in her perfect cunt, knuckles grinding into her as I stroke her through it, and feel something thin and taut brush my fingertips. The corner of my mouth curves.

I stroke her clit with my free hand, keeping her hovering, and tug gently at the hidden prize until she gasps at the unexpected sensation. My voice is low, rough silk. "You don't need this anymore, do you, wife?"

Her head shakes wildly, hair spilling across the altar. "No," she breathes, the word breaking apart on a moan.

"You want to have my baby, don't you?" I press, curling my fingers so deep, I touch her cervix, making her sob with pleasure.

"Yes... please," she blurts, greedy, desperate. The way she says it makes something feral snap inside me.

I tug the strings slowly, letting her feel every millimeter drag through her tender channel. She cries out at the sharp, alien ache of it, hips jerking forward against the altar as if she can get away from the pull—but she is chained, and with the little she can move, I keep her pinned, my other hand splayed over her lower back, forcing her to still.

The small device slides free into my palm at last. I tilt it into her line of sight so she knows exactly what I've taken.

"Mine now," I growl, savoring the way her eyes flash with pain and something darker, before tossing it aside like it's nothing but trash between us.

I have another mission now, I'll fuck her ass another day. I press my cock into her from behind, the stretch deep and claiming, and the altar's unyielding stone digs into her hips, holding her as much as I do. Her gasp fractures into a cry that's equal parts pleasure and pain, echoing up into the rafters.

"Now you're my beautiful bride—my wife," I growl, each word punctuated by a slow, merciless thrust that drives her forward against the cold surface. "I want to watch your belly swell with my child. I want everyone to see the life we made, to know you carry *me* inside you in every way."

Her fingers curl against the stone, chains rattling as she writhes under me. I set a brutal, relentless pace, my hips slamming into her beautiful cunt with the single-minded intent of keeping her here—bent over this altar, mine—in this beautiful, brutal ceremony for as long as possible. She moans with each impact, her voice breaking when I reach deeper, stretching her until her body trembles. I'm determined to last the longest I ever have with her, to keep her in this moment until she can't remember the world beyond it.

The air is thick with sweat, sex, and the faint copper scent of our blood, each breath we take a vow renewed.

When I finally let go—after slowing and pausing so many times, I've probably been fucking her for an hour—it's with a guttural growl, spilling into her in long, claiming pulses that leave no doubt she's been bred in every sense of the word.

I stay buried in her, refusing to let her body close around nothing, keeping my cock deep until I soften inside her. Only then do I pull back, and when I feel the first warm leak of my seed against her thighs, I scoop it up with my fingers and shove it back into her tight, spent heat.

"All of it stays in you, wife," I rasp, my voice edged with obsession. "I'll fuck you and fill you like this, over and over, every day, until I know you're carrying a piece of me."

My tone softens just enough to twist the knife in a different way. "You'll be an amazing mother, *ma colombe*. I'll give you a child who knows they were made from nothing but obsession and love."

After, I unfasten the chains one by one, my fingers lingering to trace and kiss the deep marks they've left on her wrists. I smooth her hair back from her sweat and tear-soaked face, cupping her cheek, letting her catch her breath while my thumb strokes along her jaw.

Then I gather her up from the altar, cradling her against my chest as I carry her out of the church into the cold air.

The wind bites at us, but I shield her with my body, murmuring soft, possessive things against her temple as we walk.

***

BACK AT THE CABIN, I take my time with her like I've never done for anyone except her. I kneel beside the bed and clean each of her wounds with deliberate care, watching her face for the smallest flinch, soothing every wince with a kiss.

I warm her body with blankets fresh from the hearth and the constant press of my own skin, pulling her against me so she steals my heat. I smooth the hair back from her damp temple, trace the curve of her cheek with my thumb, and tilt her chin to press soft, claiming kisses to her mouth between sips of water I hold to her lips.

The marks on her wrists—angry, raw—get my slowest attention; I kiss them until she sighs, knowing they'll bear the memory of today for a long time. My voice stays low, telling her she's mine, that she's safe, that I'll never leave her.

And in my head, I know why she's different—why she's dangerous to me. I've never cared before how I left a woman, never once stayed to see them breathe easy after I was through. But with her, I *need* to. By the time she drifts off, she's curled into me, one hand fisted in my shirt like she can't let go. She won't have to. I intend to keep her.

When she wakes, she says she needs to shower and I release her reluctantly and move to make her breakfast.

Sunlight filters through the curtains, warm and golden, spilling across the table where I've already set our very late breakfast. She pads in wearing one of my shirts, hair still damp from the shower, eyes softer than I've *ever* seen them.

Again, my gaze catches on the faint, raw marks circling her wrists—evidence of the chains, of me. Pride twists with something almost like regret in my chest, knowing I put them there—and knowing I'd do it again.

I pull out a chair for her and set down a plate piled high with thick slices of American-style French toast, dusted with powdered sugar, drizzled in syrup. A glass of fresh orange juice sits beside a flute of mimosa.

She takes a bite, eyes closing at the taste, and I can't stop watching her.

"Yesterday," I begin, voice steady, "men came for you." Her fork stills. "They won't try again—not those ones. But there will be others. Which is why we're leaving."

Her brow furrows, confusion mixing with trust. "Leaving?"

"I'm taking you to France," I say simply, pouring her another mimosa. "Private plane. We'll be gone before midnight."

She swallows hard, eyes shimmering. Her gaze flickers from my face to her plate, then back again, searching me like she's trying to read every unspoken thing between us. She sets her fork down slowly, fingers brushing over the faint marks on her wrists as if only now noticing them. I watch the way her breath catches, the way her lips part like she wants to speak but doesn't.

Finally, I add, "I'm not your savior, *ma colombe*. I'm your sentence. And I love you too fucking much to set you free."

I tilt my head, letting the silence stretch until she gives me that small, shaky smile that tells me she's still with me—still mine—and I slide my hand into my pocket.

"And one more thing." I place a small velvet box on the table and open it to reveal a diamond ring—bright, brilliant, unmistakable. "It wasn't sanctioned by the government, but you are my wife. You always will be."

Her lips part, and the first tear spills before she can stop it. I take her hand, slip the ring onto her finger, my thumb stroking over her knuckles. "Now the rest of the world will know it too."

She presses her free hand to her mouth, a sob breaking into a laugh as more tears fall.

"I love it," she whispers, voice trembling. "I love you."

I lean in, kissing her slowly, tasting the sweetness of syrup and the salt of her tears.

"Good," I murmur against her lips. "Because you're mine. Always."

12

THE BRIDE WORE BLACK

SAVANNAH

A MONTH LATER, WE had traded the ruin of the church for the vines of Bordeaux. Spring had broken here—blossoms spilling over stone walls, the vineyard rows thick with new green.

This part of France smells like earth and wine and the faint trace of woodsmoke drifting from chimneys in the village beyond the hills.

From my balcony, the vineyard stretches in every direction—a quilt of deep green and early-gold, the grapes swelling under the last heat of summer. The air is cooler here, cleaner, but I think the difference is more than geography. I breathe easier because I'm not holding my breath anymore.

The girl who used to live inside me—the one with pearl necklaces and polite smiles and a life measured in optics—was already gone, but Leon buried her completely the night he chained me to that altar.

And in her place?

I became his bride in black lace.

I don't know if anyone would call me free. Maybe I'm not. But I love this cage, if it is one.

I sit on the balcony like a queen on her dais, the rows of vines below my kingdom. His hand rests on my shoulder, warm, anchoring. The cage became a throne—and the throne is ours.

***

THE HOUSE IS OLDER than the vineyard, all weathered stone and dark beams polished by decades of sun, each creak and shadow telling a story older than either of us.

In the mornings, the housekeeper sweeps up the dust from the day before while the scent of yeast and honey drifts from the kitchen, and I find fresh bread still warm from the oven.

The cook hums as she works, plating lunches as if every day were a celebration.

Three older men tend the vines, their shirts sun-bleached and hands permanently stained with earth; they nod when we pass but never ask questions. I don't ask how much they know about Leon, and they don't ask me who I was before, as if we've all agreed some histories are better left untouched.

Sometimes I roam the corridors before the world wakes, my fingertips brushing over cold stone, pausing at the windows where sunlight spills over the endless rows of grapes.

When the light is soft, I slip outside barefoot, trailing my hands along the leaves, feeling the cool dew kiss my skin. Some days, I carry my cello into the open air and play until my fingers ache and my shoulders tremble. The sound rises—low, mournful, alive—then dissolves into the hills as though the land itself swallows my secrets.

He listens, I know he does. Sometimes from the porch with coffee in hand, the steam curling in the cool air, sometimes from the shadows like the predator he is, watching without interrupting, letting me feel the weight of his gaze.

At least once a week I still talk to Lise—my lifeline glowing through a computer screen. She's my litmus test, part of the foundation I've managed to hold onto. Her respect for my autonomy, even if not my choices, steadies me.

When he's gone on contracts, the air feels thinner, my lungs greedy for something they can't draw in. It's as if part of the world leaves with him. I never ask where he goes, and I never need to. I know what it costs him—the weight on his shoulders, the unspoken stains on his hands before they touch me.

And I feel safer when those hands are here, the danger in them turned into a shield that no one else could ever offer me.

***

TODAY, HE'S HOME.

I hear his boots on the tile before I see him. That sound has become my favorite—steady, heavy, inevitable. He steps into the kitchen, the late sun gilding the edges of his hair, his shirt sleeves rolled up, forearms bare and marked by the faint ghosts of old scars.

"*Ma reine*," he says, and even now, months later, my stomach still clenches when the French slides off his tongue. *My queen.*

I lean back against the counter as he closes the space between us. His hands settle on my hips, thumbs stroking slow circles. There's still that constant thread of danger in him, but I've learned it's not something I want to cure. It's the part that keeps me warm.

"I was thinking," he murmurs against my temple, "we'll bottle the new vintage next month. You'll help me choose which cases to keep."

It's domestic in a way that should feel absurd coming from him, but here, it doesn't. Here, it feels like another vow.

His gaze drops to my mouth. "Do you miss it?"

"The States?"

He shakes his head, brushing his thumb over my bottom lip. "Freedom."

I smile at that—slow, certain. "I wasn't free and I don't want that kind of freedom anymore."

"What do you want?"

I rise on my toes, my lips brushing his. "You."

His mouth curves, but there's nothing soft about the way his hands tighten on me. "Good answer."

***

AT NIGHT, THE VINEYARD goes black, the only light the pale wash of the moon spilling over the rows like a witness.

Inside, he turns our bedroom into another kind of darkness—one made of leather, steel, and his will. Some nights, he binds my wrists to the headboard with his belt so tightly the skin beneath warms and throbs, holding me there until my arms ache and my breath hitches at every movement. Other times, he pins me face-down across the bed, his weight an unyielding brand, the cool kiss of his knife tracing lazy, deliberate lines down my spine before pressing just enough to make my pulse roar in my ears. I shiver, knowing the blade could break more than thin skin at his whim, and it thrills me.

On nights when his patience runs thinner, the cold press of a gun barrel finds the tender skin of my inner thigh, a reminder that he could end me and he's the only reason I'm alive.

My heartbeat stutters into a sprint, and before the fear can bloom into anything real, his mouth is on mine—rough, consuming, claiming like he intends to swallow every protest I'll never make.

He fucks me with the windows open, the scent of grapes, earth, and fresh air drifting in, mingling with the salt of my sweat and the copper ghost of earlier games. His grip is bruising, his pace merciless, each thrust a silent command to remember who I belong to.

Between filthy words in my ear, he tells me truths I can feel down to the marrow—that I breathe because he allows it, that my body is his cathedral and he'll desecrate and worship it in equal measure, that I will always be his and no one will ever take me from him without dying for the attempt.

The sound of his voice in those moments is as binding as the leather around my wrists, as sharp as the knife against my skin, and as final as the click of a safety sliding off in the dark.

And the truth—the one I used to think I'd never speak—is that I don't want anything else.

I didn't escape the devil.

I married him.

And I love him.

EPILOGUE

SAVANNAH

THE VINEYARD IS HEAVY with summer, the grapes fat and sweet on the vine. I walk barefoot between the rows, my dress brushing my legs, one hand on the gentle swell of my belly. It's still small enough to hide if I wanted to—but I don't. I want the whole world to know.

The air is thick with lavender and sun-warmed soil, and every breath feels different now. Heavier. Fuller. I used to think "full" was about a life packed with events and obligations. Now it's about moments like this—morning light cutting over the vines, a cello resting on its stand inside, the weight of him always somewhere close.

I feel him before I hear him. That low shift in the air, the pull of something dangerous and inevitable. My pulse jumps, but not in fear. *Never* in fear.

He steps into the path between the vines, his shirt sleeves rolled up, forearms golden in the light, eyes locked on me like I'm the only thing worth looking at. The look in them says he's already counted every breath I've taken since he left this morning. His gaze drops to my stomach, and his mouth curves in that slow, sinful way that makes me ache everywhere at once.

I stop walking. Wait for him to close the distance. And when his hands come to rest low on my hips—strong, warm, claiming—I think of the girl I was before him. That girl would have called this insane and a cage. The woman I am now calls it home.

His hand slides over my belly, a brand as certain as the blood vows we made.

✳✳✳

LEON

HER BELLY IS STILL small, but I see it. I feel the proof that my mark isn't just on her skin or in her blood anymore. It's alive, growing—permanent.

She smells like sun and summer and my fucking obsession. I slide my palms over her hips, then lower until I can feel the curve where her body is changing, my thumbs stroking slow circles into the silk of her dress.

"*Ma femme*," I murmur, my lips brushing her temple, "you breathe because I let you. And now you're breathing for two."

Her smile is soft, but the grip she has on my shirt is not—hooking, dragging me close, like she knows exactly what I need. I lower myself, sinking to one knee in the dirt between the vines. My hands cup her belly, thumbs meeting at the center, my head bent as if in prayer—though the only god I've ever believed in is standing right in front of me.

I press my mouth to where our child sleeps beneath her skin... and bite. Just enough for her to gasp, her fingers tangling in my hair, holding me there. I taste the faint salt of her sweat, the clean sweetness of the dress, and underneath it—the heat of her, the thrum of her pulse, the promise of the life we made.

She tugs at me, thinking I'll stand. I don't. I fist the hem of her dress and push it up, up, until the sun is spilling over the curve of her ass. My hands grip her thighs, forcing them apart. The air between the vines is warm, but her cunt is hotter, already wet for me.

"Still mine," I growl against her skin, sliding her panties to the side and two fingers inside her without warning.

She gasps, half-outrage, half-want, her hips rolling forward into the pressure. My fingers fuck her slow at first, feeling the way her body clutches at me like it's been waiting all day. My thumb circles her clit, my mouth finding the soft skin above her belly again, marking her in a ring of bruises and bites.

Before she can catch her breath, I hook an arm behind her knees and another around her back. She makes a startled sound as I lift her, turning to lay her down in the strip of sunlit grass between the vines. The soil is warm beneath her, the scent of crushed green and ripe grapes wrapping around us like the walls of our own private chapel. Her hair fans out across the ground, the silk of her dress bunched high on her hips, her belly a perfect curve between us.

I kneel between her thighs, spreading them wide so I can look my fill at her beautiful pink cunt.

"Perfect," I murmur.

My knife is already in my hand—not for harm, just for truth. The blade catches the sun before I turn it flat and drag the cool steel slowly up the inside of her thigh, leaving goosebumps in its wake. At the soft flesh near her hip, I make the lightest cut—just enough for a bead of red to bloom. She exhales sharply, her eyes locked on mine.

I lower my head, licking the warm line of blood away before it can fall, savoring the taste of her in this new, heady mix—copper and salt, heat and life. "*Ma colombe,*" I murmur against her skin, "even your blood is sweeter carrying mine inside you."

The knife drops harmlessly to the grass. My hands are on her now, parting her as I lower my mouth, tongue dragging through her slick heat until she moans loud enough to startle a bird from the vines. I devour her until she's trembling, then replace my mouth with my fingers so I can make her taste the arousal off them, groaning low.

"Wetter than I thought, *ma colombe.*"

My zipper drops as she licks my fingers clean.

"*Ma parfaite petite pute. Mon ange déchu,*" I praise, because she is my perfect slut and my fallen angel.

She makes a small, broken sound when she feels the blunt head of my cock press against her entrance—but

I wait for her to look at me. I'm looking down at her, watching her pupils blow wide, watching the moment she gives me everything all over again.

I press in, slow but unyielding, my hand splayed below the rise of her belly, so she feels every inch I take. She tightens around me, greedily clenching, and I start to move—deep, deliberate thrusts that rock her against the earth. One hand finds her clit, the other stays firm under the swell of our child, holding her exactly where I want her.

"Feel that?" I breathe, my mouth at her ear. "That's me inside you. I'll fuck you every day while you're pregnant. So I make sure neither of you ever forget who you belong to."

She breaks first, crying out as her release clenches tight around me, pulling me under with her. I spill deep, grinding forward to keep it all inside her. I don't pull out quickly. And when I do, my hand cups her between the legs, holding my seed in her, feeling the slow, hot leak against my palm.

I bend over her, my mouth to her belly, my voice a vow carved in stone.

"Don't worry, little one," I murmur, though I'm speaking to both of them—Savannah and the life inside her. "Daddy already killed the world for your mother..."

I give her one last bruising thrust of my fingers, a promise punctuated with my breath against her skin.

"...I'll do worse for you."

THE END

Maelana Nightingale's Works

Sign up for my newsletter for updates on the newest releases!

Fighting For Evangeline
Dark Romance | A rescue/MMA/felon romance
A story of survival after domestic violence

The Vallyn Duet | Vallyn in Chains | Vallyn Unchained
Dark Romance | A stalker turned rescue romance
Trauma recovery and support (hurt/comfort)
The Vallyn Duet explores the depths of trauma, the complexities of recovery, & the resilience needed to rebuild. Graphic violence & emotionally intense themes are integral to the story-please read the author's note before diving in.

The Unbinding Trilogy : Unbinding Desire, Unbinding Fate, & Unbinding Forever
The Unbinding Omnibus With Bonus Content
Polyamory Romance | MFMMMM Why Choose
Contemporary Romance

Fated Love Saga Books One & Two
Classic Romance | Sweet But Steamy | Standalone
Interconnected Saga | Later in Life | Gen X
Love After Divorce | Workplace Romance

Roll For Love Trilogy
MMMFM Why Choose Polycule | Contemporary
Romance | D&D Coded | Romantic Comedy

The Prophecy of Vyrdanor Book Saga
Epic Romantic Fantasy | Coming of Age Fantasy |
Royalty & Political Reckoning | Plot Twists | Unique
Magic System & Pantheon

For a full list of Maelana's work please visit her website
www.maelananightingale.com